'Extraordinary masterpieces of the twentieth century'
– John Banville

'A brilliant writer'   – India Knight

'Intense atmosphere and resonant detail . . . make Simenon's
fiction remarkably like life'   – Julian Barnes

'A truly wonderful writer . . . marvellously readable – lucid,
simple, absolutely in tune with the world he creates'
– Muriel Spark

'Few writers have ever conveyed with such a sure touch, the
bleakness of human life'   – A. N. Wilson

'Compelling, remorseless, brilliant'   – John Gray

'A writer of genius, one whose simplicity of language creates
indelible images that the florid stylists of our own day can
only dream of'   – *Daily Mail*

'The mysteries of the human personality are revealed in all
their disconcerting complexity'   – Anita Brookner

'One of the greatest writers of our time' – *The Sunday Times*

'I love reading Simenon. He makes me think of Chekhov'
– William Faulkner

'One of the great psychological novelists of this century'
– *Independent*

'The greatest of all, the most genuine novelist we have had
in literature'   – André Gide

'Simenon ought to be spoken of in the same breath as
Camus, Beckett and Kafka'   – *Independent on Sunday*

ABOUT THE AUTHOR

Georges Simenon was born on 12 February 1903 in Liège, Belgium, and died in 1989 in Lausanne, Switzerland, where he had lived for the latter part of his life. Between 1931 and 1972 he published seventy-five novels and twenty-eight short stories featuring Inspector Maigret.

Simenon always resisted identifying himself with his famous literary character, but acknowledged that they shared an important characteristic:

> My motto, to the extent that I have one, has been noted often enough, and I've always conformed to it. It's the one I've given to old Maigret, who resembles me in certain points . . . 'Understand and judge not'.

Penguin is publishing the entire series of Maigret novels.

GEORGES SIMENON

Maigret Defends Himself

Translated by HOWARD CURTIS

PENGUIN BOOKS

PENGUIN CLASSICS

UK | USA | Canada | Ireland | Australia
India | New Zealand | South Africa

Penguin Books is part of the Penguin Random House group of companies
whose addresses can be found at global.penguinrandomhouse.com.

First published in French as *Maigret se défend* by Presses de la Cité 1964
This translation first published 2019
002

Set in 12.5/15 pt Dante MT Std
Typeset by Jouve (UK), Milton Keynes
Printed and bound in Great Britain by Clays Ltd, Elcograf S.p.A.

ISBN: 978–0–241–30406–8

www.greenpenguin.co.uk

Penguin Random House is committed to a
sustainable future for our business, our readers
and our planet. This book is made from Forest
Stewardship Council® certified paper.

Maigret Defends Himself

1.

'Tell me something, Maigret . . .'

A little phrase the detective chief inspector would remember later, but which hadn't struck him at the time. Everything was familiar – the setting, the faces, even the movements of the people involved – so familiar that he had stopped paying attention. It had happened in Rue Popincourt, a few hundred metres from Boulevard Richard-Lenoir, at the apartment of the Pardons, where the Maigrets had been in the habit of coming for dinner once a month for several years now.

And once a month, too, Dr Pardon and his wife came for dinner at Maigret's apartment – an opportunity for the two women to indulge in a friendly competition as to who cooked the best stew.

As usual, they had lingered at the table. The Pardons' daughter Solange, pregnant for the second time, looked like a balloon and seemed to be apologizing for being ungainly. She had come to spend a few days with her parents while her husband, an engineer in the eastern suburbs of Paris, was attending a conference in Nice.

It was June. The day had been stifling, and the evening was stormy. Through the open window, the moon could occasionally be glimpsed between two black clouds, which it fringed for a moment in white.

Following a tradition established at the very first dinner, the ladies had served the coffee and were now sitting at the other end of the lounge, talking in low voices, leaving the two men to have a private conversation. This was also the doctor's waiting room, and well-thumbed magazines lay piled up on a pedestal table.

Actually, there was one small detail that differed from the other times. While Maigret was filling and lighting his pipe, Pardon had disappeared for a moment into his consulting room and returned with a box of cigars.

'I shan't offer you one, Maigret.'

'No, thanks . . . So you're smoking cigars now?'

He had never seen Pardon smoke anything other than cigarettes. After a brief glance at his wife, Pardon murmured:

'It's her doing.'

'Because of all these articles about lung cancer?'

'They've made quite an impression on her.'

'Do you believe them?'

Pardon shrugged.

'Even if I did . . .'

He added in a low voice:

'Outside, I confess I . . .'

He cheated. At home, he forced himself to smoke cigars, which didn't suit him, but elsewhere he smoked cigarettes, secretly, on the sly, like a schoolboy.

He was neither tall nor fat. His brown hair was starting to turn silver and his face bore the marks of a tiring life. The evening seldom finished without an anxious phone call from a patient and Pardon apologizing for having to leave his guests.

'Tell me something, Maigret . . .'

He had said this hesitantly, with a touch of shyness.

'We must be about the same age . . .'

'I'm fifty-two.'

Pardon knew that: he was Maigret's doctor and must have his records.

'Three years away from retirement. In the police, when you reach fifty-five, they expect you to go fishing . . .'

A tinge of sadness. Sitting by the window, the two men occasionally received a breath of cool air and glimpsed a flash of lightning in the sky, unaccompanied by the noise of thunder. There were a few lighted windows in the buildings opposite, figures passing behind those windows, and an elderly man leaning on his elbows at the window of a dark room who seemed to be staring at them.

'I'm forty-nine. At school, three years' difference matters. Not at our age . . .'

Maigret could not have foreseen that the details of this idle conversation would one day come back to haunt him. He liked Pardon. He was one of the few men he enjoyed spending an evening with.

Pardon continued, still searching for words:

'You and I have pretty much the same experience of people. Many of my patients could become clients of yours.'

It was true: in this overpopulated neighbourhood, you met all sorts, the best and the worst.

'I'd like to ask you a question.'

His embarrassment was plain to see. They were friends, of course, just as their wives were friends, and yet they were reluctant to tackle certain subjects. They had never, for instance, discussed politics or religion.

'In the whole of your career,' Pardon continued, 'have you ever encountered a truly wicked criminal . . . I mean . . .'

He was once again searching for words, making an effort to clarify his thoughts.

'A conscious criminal, one who's responsible for his own actions, and acts out of pure spite, because that's his vice, as some might put it . . . I'm not talking about those who mistreat children, for example. They're almost all coarse creatures whose mental age is barely above ten, people who feel uncomfortable in an adult world and become heavy drinkers . . .'

'So basically you're talking about a pure criminal?'

'Pure or impure . . . Let's say a total criminal.'

'As defined by the penal code?'

'No. As defined by you.'

Screwing up his eyes, Maigret looked at his friend through the smoke from his pipe, concentrating above all on the cigar that Pardon held at an awkward angle, the ash from which, growing too long, was about to fall on the carpet. He finally smiled, and the doctor, embarrassed, now also looked at the cigar.

They understood each other. It was this business of cigars and cigarettes that had been bothering Pardon, a doctor who mostly treated the working classes, and had led him, perhaps unconsciously, to ask his question.

He was forty-nine, as he had just said. Every day for more than twenty years, he had treated dozens of patients who looked at him as if he were God and expected everything from him: health, life, advice, a solution to their problems.

He had saved the lives of men, women and children. He had helped others to accept their fate. Every day, he was called on to make rapid decisions that were as irreversible as those of a trial judge.

Because she had read some newspaper articles, his wife had asked him to give up cigarettes, and he hadn't felt as if he could upset or worry her by refusing. So when he was at home, he forced himself to puff awkwardly at a cigar that probably tasted awful.

But as soon as he was outside, at the wheel of his car on the way to see a patient in pain, he would light a cigarette, his hand shaking with guilt.

Maigret did not immediately answer the question his friend had asked. He had almost replied:

'What about you?'

That would have been too easy.

'If I'd had the misfortune to become a magistrate,' he began in a hesitant voice, 'or if I was called to be a juror in a criminal trial, I wonder . . . No! I'm certain I couldn't bring myself to judge a man.'

'Whatever the crime?'

'It's not the crime that matters. It's what goes on, or what went on, inside the person who committed it . . .'

'So you've never dealt with a case in which you would have condemned the person without hesitation?'

'Because of what you call wickedness? At first sight, yes. I've had people in my office I couldn't stop myself from slapping. Then, as I investigated further . . .'

That was where the conversation had ended as far as that subject was concerned, because one of the wives had approached, Maigret couldn't remember which.

'A little armagnac?'

It was Pardon's turn to throw Maigret a brief glance.

'No, thank you.'

'By the way, when was the last time I gave you a check-up?'

'About a year ago.'

There was a roll of thunder, which seemed to pass from rooftop to rooftop, but the rain they had been expecting for several days was still holding off.

'Shall we go into my consulting room for a moment?'

Pardon's daughter's first-born was sleeping there in a folding cradle.

'Don't worry, he's a deep sleeper. Although only until five in the morning, unfortunately! Now let's check your blood pressure . . .'

Maigret took off his jacket, then his shirt, leaving himself bare-chested. Pardon had naturally assumed the grave and somewhat distant manner of the medical practitioner.

'Breathe in . . . Deeper . . . Breathe through your mouth . . . Good . . . Lie down here and loosen your belt . . . I don't suppose you've made up your mind to work less, at a slower pace, as I advised you?'

'What about you?'

'I know, I know . . . Are you on a diet?'

Maigret shook his head.

'What about wine, beer, spirits? Have you reduced your intake?'

'The only result of that is that I feel ashamed when I have a glass of beer or calvados. Between cases, I can go for days on end having just a little wine with my meals. But then I go into a bar to keep an eye on the house opposite, I breathe in the sharp smell typical of a Parisian bistro and . . .'

Like Pardon with his cigarettes. Yet both of them were grown men!

The Maigrets had walked home via Rue du Chemin-Vert, as was their habit.

'What did he say about you?'

'He says I'm fine.'

This, of course, was the moment the sky chose to let loose on Paris all the water accumulated during weeks of heat.

'Shall we take shelter in a doorway?'

All this was ancient history. It was now ten days since the Maigrets had had dinner at the Pardons'. It was hot again. People were starting to leave for their holidays. In his office, Maigret was working without a jacket, with the window wide open, and the Seine glinted blue-green, like the sea on certain windless mornings.

At 10.30, as he was going through his colleagues' reports, Joseph, the elderly clerk, knocked at the door in a way that everyone in the house recognized. He came in without waiting for a reply and placed an envelope on Maigret's desk.

Maigret was surprised to see the engraved letterhead: *Office of the Prefect of Police*.

Inside was a card.

Detective Chief Inspector Maigret is requested to appear at the Office of the Prefect of Police at 11 a.m. on 28 June.

Maigret's cheeks turned red, as they had at school whenever he was called to the headmaster's office. 28 June . . . He looked mechanically at the calendar. It was indeed Tuesday 28 June. And it was 10.30. The summons hadn't arrived in the mail but had been delivered by hand.

He had been in the Police Judiciaire for more than thirty years, and the head of the Crime Squad for ten years, but this was the first time he had been summoned like this.

He had seen about a dozen prefects come and go and had been on more or less good terms with them, although some had stayed in the post for so little time that he hadn't even had the opportunity to speak to them.

Others would call him on the telephone and ask him if he would be so good as to come to their office, and it was almost always to be given a delicate and usually not very pleasant assignment: to get the son or daughter of a highly placed figure – if not the highly placed figure himself – out of an embarrassing situation.

His first reaction was to go straight to the commissioner, who must know what this was about. That morning, though, during the daily briefing, he hadn't said anything to Maigret, had behaved as he normally did, seemingly distracted, asking the odd question as if he didn't attach any importance to it.

He had only been in his post for three years, and when he was appointed he had no experience of the police, except, perhaps, through novels. He was a high-ranking civil servant who had worked in a number of different ministries.

Maigret remembered the days when the commissioner of the Police Judiciaire was chosen from among the detective chief inspectors. There had been a time when his colleagues had teased him, telling him he would end up as the big chief himself.

Now, as he walked through the inspectors' room with an anxious air, he told everybody:

'If anyone asks for me, I'm seeing the prefect.'

Two of his men at least looked up in surprise. Lucas and Janvier, who knew him better than the others, had sensed the anxiety and bad humour in Maigret's voice.

His pipe clenched between his teeth, he descended the big dusty staircase, went out the main entrance, waved at the officers on guard duty, walked along Quai des Orfèvres for a short distance and turned the corner of Boulevard du Palais.

Before facing the boss, he very nearly went into the bar opposite to have a drink – anything: beer, white wine, an aperitif of some kind – and it was only now that for the first time he remembered the last dinner at the Pardons', the business of the cigarettes, the consultation next to the folding cradle.

The guards recognized him. He entered the lift.

'The prefect's office.'

'Have you been summoned?'

He showed the letter reluctantly. Not just anyone could enter. He was led to a waiting room he knew well.

'Please wait.'

As if he had a choice! The prefect was also a newcomer. Two years on the job. A young man. That was the fashion. He wasn't yet forty but had been to the École Normale Supérieure and had then amassed enough diplomas to be put at the head of any department of the civil service.

The new broom, as the newspapers had nicknamed him after his first press conference. Yes, just like film stars, prefects now gave press conferences, always making sure there were TV cameras present.

'Gentlemen, Paris has to be a clean capital, and to achieve that, it's essential to give it a clean sweep. Too many people in the last few years, too many private interests have interfered in . . .'

11.05 . . . 11.10 . . . 11.15 . . . The clerk with his silver chain was dozing at his pedestal table, occasionally throwing Maigret an indifferent glance. He had been in service almost as long as Maigret himself.

A bell rang shrilly. The clerk rose reluctantly, half opened the door, gave a hand signal, and Maigret at last entered the big, green-carpeted Empire-style office.

'Please take a seat, detective chief inspector.'

A soft, pleasant voice; a thin, very young face, framed by fair hair. Everyone knew from the newspapers that before starting work every morning the prefect spent time at the Roland Garros Stadium, keeping himself in shape with a few sets of tennis.

He gave an impression of health and vigour – neatness, too, in his clothes, which he probably had made to measure in London. He was smiling. In all his photographs, he was smiling. His smile, admittedly, wasn't addressed to anyone in particular. It was to himself that he smiled, with modest self-satisfaction.

'Tell me something . . .'

Like Pardon the other evening, except that instead of a cigar, the prefect was smoking a cigarette. Perhaps because his wife wasn't around?

Did he have the same self-satisfied smile in his wife's presence?

'You started in the police as a young man, I think?'

'I started at the age of twenty-two.'

'How old are you now?'

'Fifty-two.'

Again just like Pardon, but presumably for other reasons.

Maigret looked his grumpiest, fiddling with an empty pipe without daring to fill it. He added, rather as if to tempt fate:

'Three years from retirement.'

'Indeed. Don't you think that's rather a long time?'

He felt himself turn red. In order not to lose his temper, he stared at the bronze adornments on the feet of the desk.

'Did you go straight into the Police Judiciaire?'

The voice still had the same softness, an impersonal softness, perhaps something he'd learned.

'In my day, you didn't start in the Police Judiciaire. Like

all my colleagues at the time, I began in a local station, the one in the ninth arrondissement.'

'In uniform?'

'I was the chief inspector's secretary. Later, I had a period on the beat.'

The prefect was studying him with a curiosity that was neither benevolent nor aggressive.

'And then you worked in several different squads?'

'The Métro, the department stores, the railway stations, vice, gambling . . .'

'It seems to have left you with pleasant memories.'

'Just like my school years.'

'I mention it because you talk about it at every opportunity.'

This time, Maigret turned crimson.

'Meaning what?'

'Unless other people talk about it on your behalf. You're very well known, Monsieur Maigret, very popular . . .'

So soft did the voice remain that it might have been thought the prefect had summoned him to offer his congratulations.

'Your methods, according to the newspapers, are quite dramatic . . .'

He stood up and walked over to the window, where for a moment he looked at the cars and buses passing the Palais de Justice. When he came back to the middle of the room, his smile – and hence his self-satisfaction – had become more pronounced.

'You're at the top of the ladder now, head of the Crime Squad, and yet you haven't abandoned the habits you picked up early in your career. You don't spend much time in your office, so I've heard.'

'No, sir, not very much.'

'You like to deal in person with tasks that would normally be handled by your inspectors.'

Silence.

'Including what you call stakeouts.'

This time, Maigret made up his mind. He gritted his teeth and filled his pipe.

'So, for example, you can be seen spending hours on end in little bars and cafés, in all sorts of places one wouldn't expect to come across a public servant of your rank.'

Was he going to light his pipe or not? He didn't yet dare. He held back, still in his armchair, while the thin, elegant prefect came and went on the other side of the mahogany desk.

'These are outdated methods, which may have had some merit in their time.'

The striking of the match made the prefect jump, but he offered no comment. For a fraction of a second, his smile faded, then returned, just the same as before.

'That old style of policing has its traditions. Informers, for example. You maintain cordial relations with people who live on the fringes of the law; you turn a blind eye to their peccadilloes and in return they give you a helping hand . . . Do you still use informers, Monsieur Maigret?'

'Like every police force in the world.'

'Do you also turn a blind eye?'

'When necessary.'

'Haven't you ever noticed that lots of things have changed since the days when you started?'

'I've seen nine commissioners and eleven prefects come and go.'

Too bad! It was a question of being true to himself, and to all his colleagues at police headquarters, the veterans anyway – the young inspectors tended to think the same way as this tennis player.

If the prefect registered the blow, nothing appeared on the surface. He could have been a diplomat. It was quite possible he might end up as an ambassador.

'Are you familiar with Mademoiselle Prieur?'

The real attack was starting. On what grounds? Maigret wasn't yet in a position to guess.

'Should I be, sir?'

'Certainly.'

'Well, it's the first time I've heard the name.'

'Mademoiselle Nicole Prieur . . . Have you also never heard of Monsieur Jean-Baptiste Prieur, Master of Requests at the Council of State?'

'No, never.'

'He lives at 42, Boulevard de Courcelles.'

'That may well be the case.'

'He's Nicole's uncle. She lives with him.'

'If you say so, sir.'

'Let me ask you, detective chief inspector, where you were at one a.m. last night.'

This time, the tone was more abrupt, and the smile had gone from his eyes.

'I'm waiting for your reply.'

'Is this an interrogation?'

'How you take it is up to you. I asked you a specific question.'

'May I ask in what capacity?'

'As your superior in the chain of command.'

'I see.'

Maigret took his time. He had never felt so humiliated in his life, and his fingers had tightened so much on the bowl of his pipe that they had turned white.

'I went to bed at ten thirty, after watching television with my wife.'

'Did you have dinner at home?'

'Yes.'

'What time did you go out?'

'I'm getting to that, sir. Just before midnight, the phone rang.'

'I assume your number is in the directory?'

'That's correct.'

'Isn't that inconvenient? Doesn't it make it possible for all kinds of people, including practical jokers, to call you directly?'

'I used to think that, too. For years, my number wasn't listed, but people always found it out in the end anyway. After changing numbers five or six times, I let it appear in the directory, like everyone else.'

'Which is convenient for your informers. They can call you directly instead of calling the Police Judiciaire, and as far as the public are concerned, you get all the credit for solving a case.'

Maigret managed to keep silent.

'So – you received a call just before midnight. How long before midnight?'

'It was dark when I answered the phone. It was a long conversation. When my wife switched on the light, it was ten to midnight.'

'Who was phoning you at such an hour? Someone you knew?'

'No. A woman.'

'Did she tell you her name?'

'Not just then.'

'You mean, not in the course of this telephone conversation you say you had with her?'

'Which I *did* have.'

'Very well! She arranged to meet you in town?'

'In a way, yes.'

'What do you mean?'

He was beginning to realize that he had been naive, although it pained him to admit it to this greenhorn with his smug smile.

'She had just arrived in Paris, where she'd never set foot before.'

'I beg your pardon?'

'I'm repeating what she told me. She added that she was the daughter of a magistrate in La Rochelle, that she was eighteen, that she felt stifled by her very strict family, especially as a school friend of hers, who's been here for a year, kept telling her about the delights and opportunities available in Paris.'

'Not very original, is it?'

'I've had confessions that were less original than that

but were genuine all the same. Do you know the number of girls, some from good families, as they say, who every year—'

'I read the statistics.'

'I grant you her story wasn't new. If it had been any newer, I might not have gone to the trouble I did. She'd left home without telling her parents, taking with her a suitcase of clothes and personal belongings as well as her savings . . . Her friend was waiting for her at Gare Montparnasse, but she wasn't alone. A man in his thirties was with her, and she introduced him as her fiancé.'

'A tall, dark stranger, the kind the fortune-tellers always mention?'

'They got into a red Lancia, and about ten minutes later stopped in front of a hotel.'

'Do you know which hotel?'

'No.'

'Nor, I suppose, in which area it's located?'

'That's correct, sir, but in my career I've known stories much more far-fetched than this one that turned out to be true. This young girl didn't know Paris. This was her first time here. A childhood friend was waiting for her and introduced her to her fiancé. She was driven down streets and boulevards she'd never seen before. They stopped at last in front of what looked like a third-class hotel, where she left her bags, and they took her out to dinner. They plied her with drinks . . .'

Maigret remembered the pathetic voice on the telephone, the simple but apt and moving words, words that – or so it seemed to him – it was impossible to make up.

'It's true I'm still a bit drunk,' she had admitted. 'I don't even know what I drank . . . "Come and see my apartment," my friend said. And the two of them took me to a kind of modern studio apartment, where I started to panic as soon as I saw the prints and especially the photographs on the walls. My friend laughed. "Is that what you're afraid of? Show her, Marco, that it's not so terrible." '

'If I understand correctly, she told you all this on the telephone, and you were listening in bed, with Madame Maigret next to you.'

'That's right, except that there may have been some details she only told me later.'

'So this continued later?'

'It got to a point where she felt she had to run away, and she found herself alone in Paris, without her luggage, without her handbag, without her money.'

'And that was when it occurred to her to phone you? Obviously, she knew your name through the newspapers. She didn't have her handbag, but she found the money to call you from a public telephone.'

'From a café, where she went in, ordered a drink and asked for a telephone token. Café owners don't usually ask to be paid in advance.'

'So you flew to her rescue. Why didn't you ask the local police to help her out?'

Because Maigret had had his doubts, but he was determined not to mention them. From now on, in any case, he would say as little as possible.

'You see, detective chief inspector, the young woman in question isn't from the provinces at all, and her version of events bears no relation to yours. Monsieur Jean-Baptiste Prieur was worried this morning when his niece didn't come to breakfast and he discovered that she wasn't in her room. She returned in a dishevelled state, almost distraught, at eight thirty this morning. The story she told had such an effect on Monsieur Prieur that he personally telephoned the minister of the interior. When I was then informed, I sent someone to take a statement in shorthand from Mademoiselle Prieur . . . You're three years from retirement, Monsieur Maigret.'

Pardon's words came back to him.

'Tell me something . . . In your career, have you ever encountered . . .'

Pure spite! Wickedness for its own sake! A wicked act committed in full awareness!

But who?

'What do you want from me, sir? My resignation?'

'I would have to accept it.'

'What's stopping you?'

'I'd like you to read the young lady's account, which has been typed up. Then I'd like you to put down in writing your version of events, just as you've told it to me. Naturally, I forbid you to bother Mademoiselle Prieur or to question anyone about her. I'll summon you again when I've received your statement.'

He walked to the door and opened it, a vague smile still on his lips.

2.

Having spurned the lift, Maigret was on the third or fourth step of the white marble staircase when the door opened again. It was the one-armed clerk, who certainly couldn't play tennis every morning.

'The prefect would like you to come back for a moment, detective chief inspector.'

He stood there for a moment, irresolute, not knowing if he should go back up the few steps or continue on his way down. He finally walked back across the waiting room, and the prefect himself opened his door to him.

'I forgot to make it clear that I don't want any rumour about this business at Quai des Orfèvres. In particular, I'll hold you personally responsible if anything leaks out to the press.'

As Maigret remained motionless, he added by way of farewell:

'I'm grateful to you.'

'Likewise, sir.'

Had he said that or hadn't he? He couldn't remember. He went back past the clerk, to whom he waved, and walked down the marble staircase, all the way this time. Outside, he was surprised to be back in the sun and the heat, among men and women in motion, the stream of cars, the colours and smells of daily life.

There was a sudden spasm in his chest and, like a man with a heart condition, he mechanically raised his hand to it and stopped walking.

Pardon had assured him it was nothing, just aerophagia. These attacks were frightening nonetheless, especially when they were accompanied by dizziness. The objects and people around him became less real, as in an out-of-focus photograph or one where the camera has moved.

At the corner of the boulevard, he walked into a café-bar, half the windows of which had a view of the riverbank. For years, he had been in the habit of dropping in here for a quick drink.

'A draught beer, inspector?'

He was having difficulty breathing. His forehead was covered in sweat, and he looked at himself anxiously in the mirror between the bottles lined up on the shelf.

'A cognac.'

He was no longer red, but pale, his gaze fixed.

'Large or small?'

'Large!' he said ironically.

Again because of Pardon. It was incredible how important that conversation, apparently so trivial, which he had had with his friend was coming to seem. Pardon had advised him to drink less, even though he himself, while smoking cigars at home to please his wife, lost no time, once he was outside, in lighting a cigarette.

'In your career, have you ever encountered . . .'

A spiteful criminal, one who committed wicked acts for their own sake.

He hadn't even smiled ironically.

'Give me another one, François.'

It was 11.40 according to the clock. It had all happened in less than half an hour, half an hour that had opened up a kind of chasm in his life. From now on, there was the past and the present, before and after. But was there an after?

His vision was still blurred. What if he fell, right here, on the tiled floor of the café, surrounded by people having their aperitif and taking no notice of him?

Come on, Maigret! No sentimentality. No childishness. How many of the men he had interrogated in his office had felt their heart beating too fast, or had had the impression it was stopping altogether? He had served them a glass of cognac, too, from the bottle kept in his cupboard.

'What do I owe you?'

He paid. He felt hot. It really was hot. The other people here were also mopping their foreheads with their handkerchieves from time to time. Why was François looking at him as if he had suddenly changed?

He didn't zigzag. He wasn't drunk. You don't get drunk on two glasses of cognac, even large ones. He waited patiently for the lights to change, then crossed and headed for the famous 36, Quai des Orfèvres.

He was no longer angry at that snotty-nosed prefect, although a little earlier he would happily have punched him in the face. In this affair, the prefect was merely a pawn.

True, he didn't like police officers of the old school. Among the heads of departments, Maigret was the last of them. He had seen the others retire one by one and had had to get used to younger faces and a different view of the profession.

Almost the only veteran left at the Police Judiciaire was

old Barnacle, an inspector who was already there when Maigret had arrived and was still in the same post, because he hadn't managed to pass a single exam.

They called him the Sniffler, because of his almost constant head cold, or else Bigfoot. He could never find shoes his size, which meant that his feet were always sore. Since they couldn't use him for more difficult tasks, he was the one they sent door to door, like a vacuum-cleaner salesman, to question the concierges, even the inhabitants of an entire street.

Poor Barnacle! Maigret had never felt so close to him. He would be leaving in three months. And Maigret?

He raised his hand to greet the men on duty and slowly climbed the stairs, stopping halfway up because he again had the feeling his heart wasn't beating regularly.

He walked into his office, closed the door behind him and looked around him as if what he was seeing was unusual, even though he knew the slightest detail. With the passing of the years, the objects had had time to become set in aspic, to come to look permanent. He was tempted to open the cupboard that contained the wash-basin and the famous bottle of cognac for clients who felt faint.

Shrugging, he entered the inspectors' room.

'Anything new, boys?'

They looked at him the same way François, the waiter in the bar, had done. Lucas stood up.

'Another raid on a jeweller's.'

'Do you mind dealing with it?'

He stood there, hovering between reality and unreality.

'Phone my wife and tell her I won't be home for lunch.

25

And before you leave, order me a few sandwiches and some beer.'

His colleagues were wondering what was going on with him. What could he tell them? He didn't know himself yet. For the first time, he was the one under attack, the one being asked to account for his actions.

He took off his jacket, opened the other half of the window and collapsed into his armchair. Six pipes were lined up on his desk, files he hadn't yet opened, documents to be signed, too, no doubt.

He chose a pipe, the biggest one, and slowly filled it. When he lit it, it didn't taste good. He had to stand to get from his jacket the papers the prefect had given him.

Someone had been sent to Monsieur Jean-Baptiste Prieur's residence on Boulevard de Courcelles to take down a statement from the young woman. That someone was probably an inspector. From which department had he been chosen?

Master of Requests at the Council of State. Maigret had a vague memory of reading the words 'Council of State' above a monumental door on Place du Palais-Royal. It was a body that was very high up in the hierarchy of government, but, like most Frenchmen, he had only a vague idea of its remit.

The Council of State, as far as he knew, ensured the constitutionality of laws and decrees and probably also decided on the admissibility of complaints by individuals and communities against the state.

Master of Requests therefore meant that the person bearing this title had the task of presenting the complaints in question to the Council, having first examined the files, and giving a considered opinion.

> Statement of Mademoiselle Nicole Prieur, 18, student, living at 42, Boulevard de Courcelles with her uncle, Monsieur Jean-Baptiste Prieur, Master of Requests at the Council of State. Statement taken at 9.30 a.m. on 28 June.

Boulevard de Courcelles: big apartment buildings facing the Parc Monceau, wide gates, chauffeurs polishing cars in the courtyards, concierges in uniform, just like the prefect's clerk.

> On Monday evening, after having dinner with my uncle, I went to Boulevard Saint-Germain to see a friend, Martine Bouet, whose father is a doctor. I took the Métro, because my uncle needed the car.

Maigret took notes. After dinner the previous evening, he had watched television with Madame Maigret, with nothing to indicate what awaited him not long afterwards.

> We spent most of the evening in Martine's bedroom, listening to the new records she had got for her birthday. Martine is crazy about music. So am I, although not quite as much as her.

How innocent and virginal it all was! Two girls in a bedroom, listening to . . . Listening to what? Bach? The latest pop songs? Jazz?

I left her about 11.30, and my first idea was to go home by Métro. Once out on the boulevard, however, I felt like walking a little, because it was a cool night, and the day had been stifling.

He tried to imagine her, in the sitting room of the apartment on Boulevard de Courcelles, dictating this statement with a self-important air. The sentences seemed straight out of a school essay. Had her uncle been present? Had there been moments when she had backtracked and corrected herself?

After a while, I turned into Rue de Seine to get to the riverside, because I love walking by the river, especially at night. That was when I realized that I had left at Martine's two records I had taken with me to play to her.

My uncle is in the habit of going to bed early, because he gets up at the crack of dawn. I knew he had only gone out for about an hour. I was afraid that Martine would call the house to say that I had forgotten my records . . .

It was possible. Anything is possible, Maigret knew that now, in a way he had never known it before. This part of the account, though, sounded less clear than the beginning.

I found myself outside a little café, where the owner was sitting by the window, reading his newspaper. I remember clearly the words painted on the front: *Désiré's*.

An old-fashioned bistro, with a tin counter, five or six polished wooden tables and quite dim lighting! I went in . . .

Maigret would soon be making his entrance, and he wondered how his character would be introduced. At that hour the previous night, he had been sleeping innocently in the bed he shared with Madame Maigret.

I immediately asked for a telephone token, and the owner stood up reluctantly, as if he did not like being disturbed. I told him to serve me a coffee at any of the tables and went into the phone booth.

Once I had Martine on the line, we chatted for a while. She wanted to know where I was. I told her that I was calling from a delightful old-fashioned bistro where there wasn't a soul, not even a cat . . . Although actually, there was a cat, a big tabby, sitting on the owner's lap . . . For a while, we discussed the possibility of her joining me, but then I told her I would not be there for long, that I wanted to walk another few hundred metres and then take the Métro.

Maigret's detective's instincts were starting to come to the fore. She must definitely have phoned her friend, because that was a detail that could be checked. She had definitely been in a bistro called Désiré's, because that was where Maigret had joined her soon afterwards. So there had been two phone calls, one to Martine, the other to Maigret.

But she had only mentioned one telephone token. Maigret was eager to know if she was going to mention a second one.

29

Our conversation lasted about ten minutes, perhaps a little more. We had only just said goodbye, of course, but two girls always find things to talk about. You think you have finished and then you launch into another subject . . .

That meant that the first telephone call hadn't been to Martine, but to Maigret, giving the latter time to get dressed, get in a taxi and reach Rue de Seine.

Next, I sat down at the table where my coffee was waiting for me. The owner had resumed his place by the window, and the cat was back on his lap. There was an evening newspaper lying on a chair, and, as I had not read it, I started looking through it while waiting for my coffee to cool down.

I have no idea how many minutes went by.

Here, too, she would have had to take into account any possible testimony on the part of the bistro owner. At that moment, she must have been wondering if Maigret would come or not, after the yarn she had spun him on the phone. The timing, at any rate, was perfect.

'Come in!' Maigret called out.

It was the waiter from the Brasserie Dauphine, bringing him a tray of sandwiches and two bottles of beer.

'Put them down there.'

He was neither hungry nor thirsty. Frowning, he went and closed the door, which the waiter had left ajar on his way out.

One detail in any case was true: the cup of coffee. And

when Maigret had got to Désiré's, there was indeed a newspaper, half open on a chair near the girl.

I did not have the feeling much time had passed, but I could not swear to it. My uncle often tells me off for having no notion of time . . . I was about to take my purse from my pocket. I was wearing a light suit with two pockets, so I had not taken my handbag with me. Another one of my faults: I am always leaving my handbag in different places. Which is why, as far as possible, I choose clothes with pockets.

Clever. That settled the matter of the supposedly stolen handbag.

It was then that a man came in, quite a tall man, with broad shoulders and a heavy face . . .

Thanks for the description!

I may be mistaken, but I have the impression that he had been looking at me through the window for a while. I vaguely remember seeing someone of the same build walking up and down the pavement.
    I thought at first that he was coming towards me, but he sat down at the next table, or rather he collapsed on to a chair and mopped his brow. I have no idea if he had been drinking, but it did occur to me.

Careful! From here on, in particular, her statement had to coincide with what the owner of the bistro would say later.

His face seemed familiar, although I could not put a name to it. Then I remembered that I had seen his photograph in the newspapers.

He seemed to read my thoughts because he said:

'You're not mistaken. I really am Detective Chief Inspector Maigret.'

That was a mistake. Maigret would never have uttered a sentence like that. But the girl had had to give a plausible explanation of why they had immediately got into conversation.

And Désiré, still sitting there on his chair, was an inconvenient witness.

In reality, he hadn't got up when Maigret came in, but had merely peered over the top of his newspaper. It was a moot point why he kept his bistro open. Perhaps out of habit? Or else to be alone and read his newspaper in peace instead of going to bed with his wife?

I am not the kind of girl who runs after stars and celebrities to get their autographs. Celebrities visit my uncle every week on Boulevard de Courcelles.

All the same, I was pleased to see a policeman at close quarters, especially the one everyone is always talking about. I had imagined him to be bigger, especially fatter. What surprised me most, at first sight, was how merry he was, and I immediately wondered if he had been drinking.

That again! And as a result, Maigret once again remembered the famous evening at the Pardons', which was definitely taking on a ridiculous degree of importance in his mind. He was being accused of drinking! And now, too, he had drunk. Two cognacs. Big ones! The waiter in the café could testify to that. And there was beer on the tray. As if defiantly, he poured himself a glass, angrily grabbed a sandwich, bit into it and immediately put it back down.

He wasn't hungry. He was fuming, plunging ever further into an unknown world in which he was playing the main role without knowing exactly what that role was.

In a nightmare, you are aware that everything is false. Even though you may believe in the reality of it for as long as you are asleep, waking up soon puts an end to the inconsistency.

Here, it was reality that was inconsistent. He wasn't asleep. He wasn't dreaming. He had in front of him a statement that wasn't some anonymous letter, or an account by a lunatic, but a perfectly official document given to him by the prefect of police in person.

And the prefect of police believed it. Was Maigret going to end up believing it as well? He remembered what had preceded that scene in the bistro. The ringing of the telephone, then the young girl's voice, the listening in the darkness, wondering if he should hang up, then Madame Maigret lighting the bedside lamp and asking:

'What is it?'

He had shrugged, still listening to the story being told in a faltering, supplicant voice.

He had still been in a solid world then: at home, in a room he had occupied for more than twenty-five years. His wife was next to him, and she, too, was quite real.

She handed him a pipe he hadn't emptied before going to bed and lit a match. She knew that whenever he was dragged abruptly from his sleep, he liked to take a few puffs at his pipe to wake himself up.

He had occupied this office for a long time, too. He had always thought it was real, and now it was already becoming less so. God alone knew what would happen when Maigret submitted his version of events to the prefect.

What were the words used by this man who had been promising for two years to sweep Paris clean and who played tennis every morning at the Roland Garros Stadium, where he was happy to be photographed?

Incidentally, he had been spiteful and unfair as far as Maigret's fame was concerned. Maigret had never looked for fame. On the contrary. How many times had his investigations been complicated by the fact that he was recognized everywhere he went? Was it his fault the journalists had created a legend around him?

Anyway, where was he? Oh, yes! The prefect had said something like:

'So just because an unknown young woman tells you a touching if rather unlikely story, you get up in the middle of the night and rush to the bistro she's indicated. Although you're head of the Crime Squad, it never occurs to you to call the nearest police station and send an inspector to deal with the matter.'

He wasn't all that wrong. In fact, Madame Maigret had said much the same thing.

'Why don't you send an inspector?'

Precisely because the matter wasn't clear-cut, because

there was something inconsistent about the story he had been told over the phone. Isn't life often inconsistent? He'd had proof of that once again, except that this time he found himself at the centre of this inconsistency.

One point to the prefect. But it wasn't the prefect Maigret was angry with, not any more. He no longer had any desire to punch him in the face. He was only a pawn in this affair and he, too, now looked like a fool.

He emptied his glass, filled another, which he put down within arm's reach, and took the time to light a pipe before once more tackling the typewritten sheets.

He ordered a white wine. The owner asked him:

'A bottle?'

He replied yes and he was brought a glass and a small bottle. He offered me some, but I told him I had just had coffee. I can't remember how he brought up his proposal. Something like:

'Most people have the wrong idea about our profession. You, too, I'd be willing to bet.

'They talk mainly about your interrogations, the confessions you finally obtain by wearing the suspect down.

'That's the end result. What matters is the routine work. For example, this evening, I'm on the lookout for a dangerous criminal I'm almost sure to find in one of the local bars.'

In spite of its pathos, the account she had given him over the phone, the story of her friend and the sinister Marco, held up rather better under close scrutiny than the words she had put in Maigret's mouth.

'You might enjoy coming with me.'

He stood up, convinced I would accept. He threw some coins on the table and, when I tried to pay my bill, the owner told me it was already settled.

I left at the same time as him.

'Are your parents waiting for you?'

'My uncle doesn't care what time I get back. He trusts me.'

'Then let's go.'

I yielded to my curiosity. I remember going along Rue Jacob, then down a little street whose name I have forgotten and into a bar where a lot of people were crowding around the counter.

I looked especially at the faces around me, wondering if the criminal the inspector was looking for was one of the customers. He handed me a glass. It was whisky. I hesitated about drinking it, but I was thirsty, because I had let my coffee get cold and it had been bitter.

I suspect my glass was refilled later without my being aware of it so that I had two drinks when I thought I was only having one. Everyone was standing shoulder to shoulder. It was hot, and the place was full of smoke.

'Let's go. The only people I've seen here are two unimportant pimps. The man I'm looking for is somewhere else.'

'I'd rather go home.'

'Give me another half-hour and I'm sure you'll have the chance to witness a dramatic arrest that'll be on the front pages of all the papers tomorrow.'

For her story to hold up, he would have needed time to get her drunk. She also had to keep things fairly vague so that it would be impossible to locate the places she claimed she had been taken. The two stories, in other words, had to coincide, each as fake as the other, but nevertheless with the same basis in reality.

The second place was in a cellar, where jazz was playing. People were dancing. I don't know the cellars of Saint-Germain-des-Prés, but I assume this was one of them. The inspector made me drink some more. I was no longer myself. I was unsteady on my legs and I thought another drink might buck me up.

After that, it gets more and more blurred, with complete gaps in my memory. Out in the street, he held me by the arm then, on the pretext that I might fall, by the waist. I tried to push him away. He took me through a door and along a dimly lit corridor. He spoke to someone through a little window, an unshaven old man with white hair.

I remember a narrow staircase, red carpeting, numbered rooms, the inspector turning a key.

I kept repeating mechanically:

'No! . . . No! . . . I don't want to . . .'

He just laughed. We were in a room, next to a bed.

'Leave me alone! . . . Leave me alone, or I'll call the—'

I could swear he replied:

'Don't forget I am the police!'

It was almost true. Not the last sentence, obviously. And the girl hadn't struggled. Nor had Maigret led her from one bar to another, or given her anything to drink.

What was true was that they'd met at Désiré's and had exchanged various words. The girl, at that point, had indeed said her name was Nicole, but she claimed that her surname was Carvet and that she was the daughter of a justice of the peace in La Rochelle. Her friend, the one who had been waiting for her at the station with Marco, was called Laure Dubuisson, and she was the daughter of a wholesale fish merchant in the same city.

'If I understand correctly, you don't know where your friend lives, or where you were taken or where you left your luggage. Last but not least, you'd be unable to recognize the building you ran away from, leaving your handbag containing your savings.'

She was still drunk, and her breath smelled of alcohol.

'The most important thing is to find you a bed for the night. Let's go.'

It was true that he had thrown some coins on the table. True, too, that once on Boulevard Saint-Germain, he had supported her by holding her arm, and that a little later, as she was swaying more, he had held her by the waist.

He knew a decent, inexpensive hotel, the Hôtel de Savoie in Rue des Écoles. Despite what Nicole said, they hadn't stopped on the way.

'How did you write to your friend if you didn't know her address?'

In a thick voice, she had replied:

'Do you think I'm lying, telling you stories? I wrote to her poste restante! Laure has always liked mysteries. When she was little, at school, she used to pretend . . .'

He couldn't remember what it was that Laure used to pretend. He was barely listening, in a hurry to get her off his hands.

It was also true that the night porter at the Hôtel de Savoie was unshaven and white-haired, and that he had held out a key and muttered:

'Second floor on the left.'

There was no lift.

'Help me to get upstairs. I can't stand up straight.'

He had helped her, and now it was hard for him to distinguish what was true from what was invented.

'I can't make it, Monsieur Maigret . . . I'm very drunk, aren't I? . . . I feel so ashamed. I'll never be able to go back to my parents now . . .'

They got to the second floor and Maigret did indeed turn the key in the lock.

'Get some sleep and don't worry about a thing. I'll sort this out tomorrow morning.'

In the room, she stumbled and fell to the floor, rolled over and made no attempt to get up again. In a few moments, she would be asleep.

He got her back on her feet and took off her shoes and her jacket. He was going to leave her like this when she moaned:

'I'm thirsty!'

He went to the tiny toilet, rinsed the tooth glass and filled it with cold water. When he returned, she was sitting on the bed trying to take off her skirt.

'My belt is hurting me . . .'

She drank, all the while giving him distressed looks.

39

'Won't you help me? If only you knew how sick I feel! I think I'm about to throw up.'

He had helped her to undress, leaving only her slip on. She hadn't thrown up.

'Well?' Madame Maigret had asked him when he had got home.

'A strange business. We'll deal with it tomorrow.'

'A pretty girl?'

'I must admit I didn't notice. She was blind drunk.'

'What did you do with her?'

'I took her to a hotel and had to put her to bed.'

'Did you undress her?'

'I had to.'

'Aren't you afraid . . .'

Madame Maigret had a sixth sense. He wasn't very satisfied either. At nine o'clock, when he got to his office, the first thing he did was call the Hôtel de Savoie. He was told that the young lady in room 32 had left, saying that Detective Chief Inspector Maigret, who had brought her, would be back to pay her bill.

Ten minutes later, the switchboard operator at the Police Judiciaire informed him that there was no justice of the peace named Carvet in La Rochelle and no Carvet in the phone book. No Dubuisson either.

3.

'*Don't forget I am the police!*'

Maigret was standing by the open window, both hands buried deep in his pockets, his jaws clenched around the stem of his pipe. He hadn't felt up to rereading Nicole Prieur's statement. For a long time, he had sat slumped in his armchair, weary and nauseous, with not an ounce of fight in him. For a long time now, he had felt as if he were already a stranger in his own office, vaguely aware of the sound of voices and the comings and goings in the inspectors' room.

He was three years from retirement. Pardon had made a point of that, too. Why? Because he thought he seemed tired? Because he had discovered something wrong while examining him, something he didn't want to tell him?

He had advised him to drink less, or even not drink at all. A little wine with meals. Soon, he would be put on a diet. Then given pills to take at specific times. He was about to enter the world of old people whose organs turn weak or faulty one after the other, just like old cars that constantly need their parts changing. Except that you can't yet buy spare parts for human beings.

He was unaware of the passing of time. The patches of sunlight on the carpet and wall of his office moved imperceptibly without his noticing.

He had no fight in him, not the slightest desire to defend himself. He accepted defeat. For a long while, he even felt a certain relief. No more responsibilities. No more exhausting evenings and nights hammering away at men whose confessions would finally bring investigations to an end.

'Don't forget I am *the police!*'

It was perhaps that little phrase that saved him. He was almost in Meung-sur-Loire already, where the house was ready to welcome him and his wife, with the garden he would cultivate, like his neighbours, the flowers and vegetables he would calmly water at sunrise and sunset, the fishing rods lined up in the shed . . .

'Don't forget I am . . .'

It was so unlike him, it sounded so fake, that a smile finally relaxed his face and he slowly began to unwind. He found himself on his feet, looking down at the sandwiches he had spurned. He took one, chewed a first mouthful and opened the remaining bottle of beer. He ate like this, standing by the window, looking at the Seine through the motionless foliage of the trees on the bank.

He was at last getting back in touch with the outside world: passers-by who were going somewhere, a young couple in each other's arms as they slowly crossed Pont Saint-Michel, stopping in the middle to watch a line of boats pass, to see the water flow by, to gaze at just anything, because the only thing that mattered was their joy in life, which they expressed by kissing.

Typewriters were clattering in the next room. The

inspectors must be looking questioningly at their chief's
door from time to time and exchanging worried glances.

He went back to his desk and read the last sentences in
Nicole Prieur's statement, because there were still two
sentences.

> He didn't take advantage of me. I guess at the last
> moment he lost his nerve.

He filled a pipe and went back to the window, stronger
now, a little gleam in his eyes. Then, after a sigh, he at last
went and opened the door to the next room.

Lucas was away. So were many of the others, scattered
through Paris. Young Lapointe was on holiday. Janvier
was typing a report. They all knew he was there, watching them, but, tactfully, they didn't dare look up, because
they knew that for Maigret to shut himself away like that,
something serious must be happening.

It was three p.m. according to the clock.

'Will you come in here, Janvier? Bring your notepad.'

Janvier was, along with Lapointe, the best at shorthand
in the team, and he quickly came into the office and shut
the door behind him. There was a question in his eyes, a
question he didn't dare formulate.

'Sit down. I'll dictate . . .'

It didn't take as long as he had thought. An hour earlier
he would have provided explanations, come up with
hypotheses. Now, he limited himself to the facts, avoiding
anything that might seem like a comment.

As he continued with his account, Janvier grew more

solemn, frowning and occasionally throwing his chief an anxious glance.

Twenty minutes sufficed.

'Type up three copies.'

'Very good, chief.'

Maigret hesitated for a few seconds. The prefect had called him back to his office specifically to advise him not to tell anyone about this business.

'Read this.'

He pushed the young woman's statement across the desk. After some twenty lines, Janvier turned red, as Maigret had turned red that morning in the prefect's office.

'Who could have . . .'

Good old Janvier! Lucas and he were Maigret's longest-standing colleagues, and the three men no longer needed words to understand each other.

Immediately, without a moment's thought, Janvier was asking the same question that Maigret had taken longer to formulate, because he was directly involved.

'Who?'

'That's what I'd like to know. Who?'

They were used to those more or less nymphomaniac, hysterical young women who periodically came to Quai des Orfèvres to spin their little yarns. There were even regulars they would see at fixed dates, like the so-called full-moon killers so beloved of the newspapers.

Maigret had, of course, envisaged that hypothesis, but a mad girl wouldn't have played her twin role without making a single mistake. Someone had taught her that twin role.

'While you type up this report, I'm going to perform an experiment, though I think I know the result in advance.'

So did Janvier, who had guessed what he meant.

'Don't mention this case to your colleagues. The boss is treating this like some sort of state secret. If you have any time left over, try to find out something about Monsieur Jean-Baptiste Prieur . . .'

As Maigret was about to leave the room, Janvier said:

'I hope you're not too worried, chief?'

'I did offer my resignation.'

'Did he refuse it?'

'He said he ought to accept it, but . . .'

'Meaning what?'

'I'm staying. As long as they don't throw me out. I'm determined to defend myself.'

A taxi took him first to Rue de Seine, where he walked nonchalantly into Désiré's. The owner was behind his counter, serving a group of plasterers in white overalls who had come in for their red wine. In a corner, a middle-aged man was writing a letter over a cup of coffee.

Désiré needed only a glance to recognize his customer from the previous night but he gave nothing away, avoided looking him in the face, began fiddling with glasses and bottles.

'A small glass of white wine. Not a bottle this time.'

The man, who had protruding eyes and a mauve complexion and seemed to be overcome by the heat, put a glass down on the tin counter and juggled with a bottle.

'Sixty centimes.'

The plasterers ignored Maigret. So did the customer writing the letter, who was having difficulties with his ball-point pen.

'Tell me something . . .'

Reluctantly, Désiré turned to him.

'Did I leave anything here last night? My umbrella perhaps?'

'Nobody left an umbrella.'

'Do you remember the girl who phoned me and then waited for me here? Did she ask you for one or two telephone tokens?'

Looking stubborn, Désiré said nothing at first, then:

'It's none of my business. I don't remember what happened last night anyway and there's no reason I should talk about it.'

'Did someone come in here this morning and advise you to keep quiet?'

The workers were suddenly listening in, turning in Maigret's direction and looking him up and down.

'It's sixty centimes,' Désiré repeated.

Maigret put a one-franc coin down on the counter and headed for the door.

'You've forgotten your change. I don't accept tips.'

Much the same thing happened at the Hôtel de Savoie in Rue des Écoles. The manageress was a plump woman with dyed red hair who still possessed a certain charm. She was in her office, next to the key rack.

'Good day to you, madame.'

It was obvious from her first glance at him that she knew who he was. He told her anyway.

'Detective Chief Inspector Maigret, Police Judiciaire.'

'Yes?'

'I brought a girl here last night, and I've come to pay her bill because she didn't have any money.'

'You don't owe me anything.'

'Did she pay?'

'It doesn't matter. You don't owe me anything.'

'Did someone come here this morning, pay her bill and question your night porter?'

'Listen, inspector, I know who you are and I have nothing against you, but I don't want to make trouble for myself. I don't know anything about the young lady or the things you're talking about. My books are in order. We've never been in trouble with the police, or with the tax inspector.'

'Thank you anyway.'

'I'm sorry I can't tell you anything else.'

'I understand.'

They had worked quickly. There was no point phoning Martine Bouet, the friend Mademoiselle Prieur had spent the evening with, listening to records. She wouldn't tell him any more than the others had. He was pretty much certain, in fact, that Nicole had indeed made a phone call to Boulevard Saint-Germain from Désiré's.

It wasn't the prefect who had set up this whole thing. He didn't much care for policemen of the old school and that was his right. He didn't particularly like Maigret, and thought the papers talked too much about him. That was his right, too.

The minister of the interior had phoned him that

morning in a panic to inform him about a story that might embarrass him, too.

These people weren't heroes or saints. They had only attained their positions thanks to intrigues which they preferred to forget and they still had to play the game to stay where they were.

So Maigret was involved in a dubious matter, even perhaps a scandal? An influential figure in the country was complaining and threatening to take the matter even higher?

All this was human. And how satisfying, for the new-broom prefect, to have someone older and more popular than he was in front of him and, in his quiet voice, tell him a few home truths!

Paris was sizzling in the sun. Many people had closed their shutters to keep a little coolness in. Here and there, men were fishing, and there were other lovers like those on the Pont Saint-Michel, two in particular, who had taken off their shoes and were dangling their bare feet above the water. They were laughing as they looked at their toes, which they were wiggling in a grotesque fashion.

'Janvier!'

'Coming, chief.'

He was busy on the telephone. When he entered Maigret's office, he brought some typewritten sheets with him. Maigret started reading them. He only read three or five lines.

'Are you sure you haven't forgotten anything?'

'I double-checked. But I'd rather you . . .'

No, Maigret had no desire to reread what he had said. He signed with a heavy quill pen, took an official envelope from his desk, wrote the address on it and rang for the clerk.

'Have this taken straight to the prefect's office . . . I'm listening, Janvier.'

'I called a friend of mine who's a lawyer and who's quite well acquainted with the upper levels of the civil service.'

'Does he know this Prieur?'

'He's a first-class jurist, one of the best around at the moment apparently. He was married, but his wife was killed in a car accident about ten years ago. His father was a ship owner.'

'In La Rochelle?'

'You guessed it.'

They both smiled. People who lie rarely make up the whole thing. The girl who had told him such a poignant story over the phone had said she was from La Rochelle. Her father was a magistrate and her friend the daughter of a wholesale fish merchant . . .

'Go on.'

'He still has a brother there who handles the ships. He himself has a personal fortune and lives in a huge apartment on Boulevard de Courcelles. Another brother, Christophe, who was married, had a daughter and lived in Morocco, killed himself in circumstances my friend doesn't know. His wife has dropped out of sight. It's believed she got married again, to an American, and lives in Texas. As for the daughter, she's the Nicole Prieur you know.'

'Anything else?'

'The girl passed her *baccalauréat* last year and is studying at the Sorbonne.'

'What kind of girl is she?'

'My friend has never met her, but his wife has seen her a few times. He'll talk to her when he gets home.'

There was no reason for Monsieur Jean-Baptiste Prieur, Master of Requests at the Council of State and eminent jurist, to harbour any hatred towards Maigret, whose name he might not even know, let alone to hatch a plot against him in which his own niece's reputation might be compromised.

'I'd give a lot for a private conversation with that girl.'

'I doubt you'll get the opportunity, chief.'

'Do you have any idea who might want to see me out of circulation badly enough to set up something like this?'

'I'm sure there are a fair number of people. Including those who've been robbing jeweller's shops in broad daylight for the past two months. There was another raid this morning, on Avenue Victor-Hugo.'

'Did they leave any trail?'

'None at all.'

'Did they shoot anyone?'

'Not that either. They calmly drove away, and nobody reacted, not even the jeweller, who was so stunned that it took him a whole minute before he sounded the alarm . . . Do you have an idea?'

'Perhaps . . . Where was I yesterday at eleven in the morning?'

Janvier knew, because he had driven the little black car.

'At Manuel's.'

'And the previous day at about the same time?'

'At Manuel's.'

'And . . .'

Three times in a week Maigret had paid a visit to Manuel Palmari, the former owner of the Clou Doré in Rue Fontaine, who was now living like a pensioner in his ritzy apartment in Rue des Acacias.

'It may be stupid, but I feel like going to see him again and asking a few questions.'

It seemed senseless, but weren't the events of the previous night just as senseless?

For thirty years, Palmari, most often called Manuel in underworld circles, had been a bigshot in Montmartre, where he had started out as a young pimp.

Had he had other activities, back in the days when Maigret, also young, had first met him? Maigret, a mere inspector then, had strongly suspected he had but had never been able to pin anything on him.

During those thirty years, many gangsters had disappeared from the Pigalle area. Some had been shot down by rivals; others, after a few years in prison, were *persona non grata*; others still ran more or less seedy inns in Marseille or Nice.

Manuel, who had soon put on weight, had found the wherewithal to buy the Clou Doré, which at the time was merely a shabby drinking hole, rather like Désiré's, except that most of the clientele were criminals.

The venue had soon been transformed into a modern bar, then into a restaurant with a few tables, where the customers, no longer just young people, would arrive in big American cars.

Maigret sometimes had lunch there, lingering until the little room decorated in red and gold emptied.

'Tell me something, Manuel . . .'

'Yes, inspector.'

'That fellow with a scar at the corner of his eye who was sitting in the corner . . .'

'You know how it is, customers come and go, I serve them food and drinks, I take their money, and what the eye doesn't see . . .'

Manuel was a born actor. He play-acted for himself as well as for others, and sometimes, pleased with his performance, winked at his listener.

'We've known each other a long time, haven't we?'

'We used to be a lot slimmer once upon a time, Monsieur Maigret!'

'And you didn't have a penny to your name.'

'It's true, I lived from hand to mouth, which proves I've never been mixed up in anything—'

'Or that you were already too clever.'

'You think I'm clever? I never had much schooling and can barely read a newspaper.'

'Manuel!'

'Yes?'

'The fellow with the scar . . .'

'All right, I get it! Look, I don't know what I can tell you about him. I know he didn't have that scar two months ago. Two months ago was March . . . And in March . . .'

In March, a fight had broken out between two gangs,

near the Pigalle fountain, and shots had been exchanged; one man had been left lying dead in the street, and two wounded men had disappeared as if by magic.

The new-broom prefect, who played tennis and had sworn to clean up Paris, didn't like informers and found the old methods repugnant.

But now, in the car driven by Janvier, Maigret was on his way to see an informer: Manuel who, three years earlier, as he was opening the door of the Clou Doré in the early hours of the morning to lower the shutters, had received half a dozen machine-gun bullets in the thigh and the stomach.

From the hospital where he had been taken, he had soon had himself moved to one of the best private clinics in Neuilly. Everyone, starting with the doctors, was convinced he wouldn't make it.

In Neuilly, too, Maigret had gone to see him several times.

'You hurt me, Monsieur Maigret. You know, your one fault, you police, is that you never believe people. There must have been two guys in the car, that's for sure, you can't hold a machine gun and drive at the same time. But, word of honour, I didn't see them, for the good reason that I had my back to them. When you're lowering an iron shutter, you have your back to the street, right?'

'You weren't lowering it yet. You'd only just opened the door.'

'But I was already turning. Think about it, you're an educated man. Some guys try to kill me. Thanks to them, I'm told I'll never walk again, I'll spend the rest of my days in a wheelchair, like a senile old man. Don't you think I'd like to see the guys who did that to me in jail?'

As Maigret had expected, he hadn't talked. A few weeks later, two young gangsters had been killed on the outskirts of Toulon, gangsters who had left Paris in a hurry soon after the shooting.

'You know how it is, Monsieur Maigret, these guys come and go for no particular reason. If you had to count those who suddenly discover that the air in Paris has got a bit unhealthy . . .'

The car went up the Champs-Élysées, around the Arc de Triomphe and along Avenue Mac-Mahon, then turned left into Rue des Acacias.

It was a quiet, wealthy area. Between the apartment blocks, there was still the occasional small private mansion with a weathered façade.

'Shall I come up with you, chief?'

'No. Find your colleague. I don't know who's on duty today.'

'Big Lourtie.'

'You'll find him on a corner somewhere. He'll be able to tell you what Aline has been doing since this morning.'

Aline was another character. In the days of the Clou Doré, she had served in the restaurant, a thin girl with untidy black hair and shiny dark eyes. Everyone knew she was Manuel's mistress, that he had met her when she was walking the streets.

At the clinic, he had obtained a little room for her that communicated with his. It was she, on his instructions, who had found a manager for the Clou Doré and who sometimes went to keep an eye on the restaurant and check the takings.

In three years, she had lost her rough edges and filled out. Her hair was no longer in a mess, and she dressed with a discreet sense of style, very much the 'little lady'.

The building was discreet and cosy. The big, silent lift had mahogany doors. Maigret got out on the fourth floor and rang at the door on the left. He waited for quite a long time before he heard the soft noise of the rubber-ized wheelchair as it came from the far end of the apartment.

'Who is it?' Manuel asked through the door.

'Maigret.'

'Again?'

The door opened.

'Come in. I'm alone. I was just dozing off when you rang the bell.'

Manuel now had beautiful silky white hair that gave his face a certain dignity. He was wearing a spotless white shirt, silk trousers and red slippers.

'Come on, now, for a man who's known me for so long, a man I've done so much for . . . No, let's not stay in the sitting room. Actually, I wonder why I have a sitting room, it's not my style, and I never have any visitors.'

He had set up a den just for himself, a little room that looked out on to the street. It contained a television set, a record player, two or three transistor radios of different sizes, newspapers, magazines and hundreds of detective novels. A red divan occupied one corner, next to an arm-chair covered in the same satin.

Manuel didn't smoke. He had never smoked. Nor did he drink.

'You know I don't like talking off the top of my head, but I warn you, one of these days I'll get angry. I'm a free citizen, with no criminal record. I pay the licence for my restaurant in Rue Fontaine, I don't cheat on my taxes. I live here like a mouse in a hole. I can't leave the apartment because of my leg, and I have to be undressed and washed like a baby, and helped in and out of bed . . .'

Knowing his man, Maigret waited for the end of this act. For the moment, Manuel was pretending to be grouchy.

'My telephone there, next to you, is being tapped. Don't tell me it's not. I wasn't born yesterday. Nor were you. I don't care if my conversations are recorded. But not leaving Aline alone, that's another matter entirely.'

'Has someone been bothering her?'

'Come on, Monsieur Maigret. You're cleverer than I am.'

'I doubt it.'

'You think so? I can barely read and write.'

His leitmotiv. He was as proud of it as other people were of their diplomas!

Maigret puffed at his pipe with a smile and murmured:

'If I was as clever as you, Manuel, you'd definitely have been behind bars for a long time by now.'

'There you go! The same old song. To get back to Aline, today it's a big fat guy who's tailing her. Yesterday, a short fellow with brown hair. Tomorrow, someone else. She can't go out to buy a couple of cutlets and some cheese without having one of your men hot on her heels. You yourself behave well, I admit that, and I like you, but that's no reason for you to come and see me almost every day like a sick relative. Why not bring me chocolates and flowers? If only you could tell me once and for all what it is you want to know.'

'Today, it's a personal matter.'

'Personal to who?'

'Do you know Nicole?'

'Nicole who? The streets of Paris are full of Nicoles. What does she do, this Nicole of yours?'

'She's studying at the Sorbonne.'

'The what?'

'The university.'

'And I'm supposed to know a girl who goes to university?'

'That's what I'm asking you. Her name's Nicole Prieur.'

'Never heard of her.'

'She lives with her uncle not far from here, on Boulevard de Courcelles. This uncle, Jean-Baptiste Prieur, is Master of Requests at the Council of State.'

Either Manuel's bewilderment was genuine, or else he was a better actor than Nicole herself.

'Are you serious? I don't even know what the Council of State is, dammit! You really think I know all these bigwigs?'

'How about Désiré, who owns a bistro in Rue de Seine?'

'First time I've heard his name.'

'Or the two lads who did a job this morning on Avenue Victor-Hugo?'

Manuel sat up in his wheelchair.

'Hold on now! If that's what you were leading up to, if

you've been sweet-talking me just to catch me out, then I'm not playing along any more. I may have been kind enough to pass you the odd tip in the past. That's because you can't own a bar in Pigalle without being on good terms with the police. I listen to the radio, like anyone else, so I know what happened this morning in the place you said. But what's it got to do with me? I haven't been out of here in three years, and hardly anyone comes to see me. Seeing that's the case, I'd be curious to know how I could be any kind of gang boss. The last time, you came to see me about another jeweller's, on Boulevard Saint-Martin. And the time before that—'

'Where's Aline?'

'Out shopping.'

'Locally?'

'No idea. If you really want to know, she went to buy some knickers and bras. Your inspector will be able to confirm that this evening.'

'Did she go out this morning?'

'This morning she went to see the dentist, just opposite. If that window over there had been open, I'd have been able to see her in the dentist's chair.'

The building opposite wasn't a block of apartments but a two-storey mansion with attics on top, built of stone that had turned dark grey. In the sun, the roof tiles had the same blue and pink glints as the Seine at certain hours of the day.

'Has she had toothache for a long time?'

'For the last three days.'

If Aline had gone to the dentist previously, Maigret

would have known it from the reports of the inspectors who had been following her for three weeks.

'What's his name?'

'Who?'

'The dentist!'

'You can see his nameplate from here. I can't read so far. She told me there was a dentist opposite, and I didn't bother with his name. What I do know is that his assistant or nurse or whatever is a tall skinny thing I wouldn't want in my bed for anything in the world . . . Listen! There's Aline coming back.'

Manuel had good hearing: in spite of the sitting room and hall separating them from the main door of the apartment, he had heard the key turn in the lock.

4.

The door to the sitting room was open, and they saw Aline walk across it with neat, rapid steps, perched on stiletto heels. She was wearing an orange linen tailored suit, her black hair meticulously styled. In one hand she held a handbag as black as her hair and in the other some paper bags, one bearing the trademark of a lingerie shop in the Lido, the other that of a store in Rue Marbeuf.

She had spotted Maigret from a distance but hadn't batted an eyelid, gave no indication that she recognized him and, when she came into the room where the two men were, she walked past him as if he didn't exist and bent down to plant a kiss on Manuel's forehead.

'So, Daddy, he's here again, is he?'

She was twenty-two, and Palmari was pushing sixty, but there was nothing filial about that 'Daddy'. In Aline's mouth, it was an affectionate pet name, and Manuel's smile seemed to say:

'You see the kind of woman she is?'

The fact was, the girl who had started on the pavements of Boulevard Sébastopol at the age of sixteen would probably now be taken in the street for an elegant bourgeois lady, the young wife of a doctor, an engineer or a lawyer.

'Pretty soon he'll be bringing his pyjamas and slippers, not to mention his toothbrush and his razor.'

She spoke without looking at Maigret, in a high-pitched voice with a strong working-class Parisian accent. She deliberately exaggerated it, just as Manuel liked putting on a performance. They were like two actors throwing each other lines they had learned, and both had their roles down pat.

She was a strange girl! As dark as she was, with her hazel eyes and brown skin, she wasn't from the South but from a little village in the Morbihan, from where she had come to Paris as a children's nanny.

She had worked for about six months for a very well-to-do couple in Neuilly who hadn't hesitated to leave her in charge of a girl of three and a baby in the cradle, even when she had started frequenting dance halls in Rue des Gravilliers and Rue de Lappe.

She had thrown her two paper bags on the divan and, still overdoing the accent, went on:

'What does he want this time?'

'Don't be rude to him, Aline. You know Monsieur Maigret is my friend.'

'Your friend, maybe. He gets on my nerves, and I hate that dirty pipe smell.'

Maigret wasn't offended and puffed slowly at his pipe as he looked at her. He suspected it was she, remembering her former employers, who had wanted this comfortable bourgeois apartment, whereas Manuel used to be content with the dark mezzanine he had occupied over his restaurant.

She probably had a desire for respectability.

'Do you know anyone who works at the Council of State?' Manuel asked her with a hint of irony.

'If he's the one asking, tell him I don't even know what that is. Look, he's starting to peer at my packages. I bet you in five minutes he'll be asking to see what's in them. Maybe he's just a pervert who gets all excited touching women's underwear.'

The telephone rang. In his wheelchair, Manuel gave a start and looked first at the phone, then at Maigret.

'Hello? . . . What? . . . Yes, he's here . . . It's for you, Monsieur Maigret.'

'What did I tell you? Next thing we know, he'll be getting his mail sent here.'

'Hello? . . . Yes . . . Go on.'

It was Janvier, phoning from a little café along the street.

'I'm calling just in case, chief. Lourtie is with me. The girl managed to lose him. When she left home, she walked straight to the Ternes Métro station, bought a first-class ticket and went down on to the platform to catch the train going in the direction of the Étoile. Lourtie followed her. When she got in the carriage, he slipped in through the other door. Just as the doors were closing, she jumped out on to the platform and Lourtie couldn't get out in time. He came back here. She's just returned by taxi.'

'Thanks.'

'Everything all right?'

'No.'

She had sat down on the divan, next to the two packages, and crossed her legs. Still looking at Manuel and not at their guest, to whom she seemed to have sworn she wouldn't speak, she said:

'That's the duty cop. They may change them, but I'm

starting to recognize their faces. Today's one is a real fatso who always looks like he's about to have a stroke.'

'Tell me, my dear . . .'

'What does he think, Daddy, we grew up together? Have you given him permission to be so familiar?'

'Shall I call you mademoiselle?'

'Wouldn't it be more polite if he called me madame?'

He was being made fun of, and Manuel, proud of the girl he had trained, looked at her with tender affection.

'I assure you, Aline, he doesn't mean you any harm.'

'Why did you shake off the inspector who was following you?'

'I suppose *he's* never changed his mind at the last minute?'

It was still Manuel she was addressing.

'My first intention was to go to the Galeries. Then, as soon as I got on the Métro, it occurred to me I could find what I was looking for just as well locally. He can have a look if he wants. He can even touch. I'll just have to wash my bras and knickers before I wear them.'

This little war had been going on since well before she had come on the scene. It had started between Palmari and Maigret when the young pimp, still thin and penniless in those days, had bought the bar in Rue Fontaine for cash. As if by coincidence, that had happened just a few weeks after a raid on a jeweller's.

For the first time, the robbers had used a technique which must have proved profitable, but which at the time had seemed extravagantly bold. Two men had smashed the shop's window with a hammer and grabbed the jewels in handfuls, heedless of the passers-by, who were too surprised to react, and of the jeweller gesticulating inside. Then they had got in a car in which an accomplice was waiting for them and plunged into the traffic.

Neither the jewels nor the men behind the raid had ever been found. Over the next two years, a dozen robberies of the same kind had taken place. Eventually, they had got their hands on one of the gang, a young man with no prior criminal record, named Génaro. He hadn't talked and had got five years.

Palmari, increasingly prosperous, turned his dive into a smart bar, then into an expensive restaurant.

'Business is good,' he merely replied whenever Maigret went and questioned him as if casually. 'I do quite well on the horses, too.'

And it was true that on Sunday he closed his establishment and set off for Auteuil, Longchamp or Vincennes, depending on the season.

Three times, the perpetrators of the jewel raids had been arrested. Almost all of them were customers of the Clou Doré. None had spilled the beans, or indicated how they were planning to shift the merchandise.

For two years, three years, four years, nothing had happened. Then there had been a succession of jewel robberies in the same style, with men whose descriptions differed from the previous ones, as if a new gang had been assembled by the boss.

'Listen to me, my dear . . .'

'There he is again with his "my dear"! Maybe you should ask him if we've ever slept together.'

'That's enough! I can come back with a warrant, or take

64

you with me now, if you prefer, and question you in my office. Do you know a girl named Nicole Prieur?'

She thought this over then again turned to Manuel.

'Do you know her? The name means nothing to me.'

'A young woman living on Boulevard de Courcelles with her uncle, who's an important figure.'

'Do you know any important people, Daddy, apart from the inspector here?'

'All right! I'll be back. I'm just going to tell you both something, and Manuel at least will understand: somewhere in Paris there are people, or one person, who have decided to get me out of the way.'

Aline opened her mouth to make another joke, but Manuel threw her a stern look to silence her. He was suddenly interested.

'You mean they're trying to kill you?'

'No. What they want is my resignation, or more precisely my forced retirement.'

'That would certainly suit a lot of people.'

Aline couldn't help exclaiming in her shrill voice:

'You bet! Starting with me!'

'Carry on, Monsieur Maigret.'

'They threw a girl my way.'

'And you took the bait?'

'No.'

'I'd have been surprised if you had. I remember trying, in the old days.'

'It comes to the same thing. They cleverly engineered quite a skilful bit of play-acting to make it look as if I'd got into a compromising position with this girl.'

'This Nicole something?'

'Yes.'

Maigret, more solemn now, looked Manuel in the eyes.

'I must be making someone very uncomfortable, someone I'm about to catch red-handed or who imagines I am.'

He paused, and Manuel, equally solemn, said:

'Go on.'

'It has to be someone very intelligent, who knows my habits and the workings of the police. Someone who feels I'm after him and thinks that by getting me out of the way he'll be left alone. Does anyone spring to mind, Manuel?'

Aline was silent, sensing that she could no longer intervene between the two men. They were entering a sphere that was beyond her.

'It could also be a pervert,' Manuel began.

'I thought of that. I also thought it might be an act of revenge. I've been through a list of the cases I've dealt with in the last few months, even over the last few years. None of the people involved had both the motive and the opportunity to set up something like that.'

'And you're asking my advice?'

'You know perfectly well the police have been snapping at your heels for some time now.'

'And that you're having Aline followed in the street. I still wonder why.'

'Maybe you'll find out one day.'

'If you're not forced to resign, if I understand correctly?'

'Precisely.'

'Meaning, you suspect me of setting you up with this girl, this niece of some bigwig . . .'

'I came to see you on the off-chance.'

There was a quite impressive silence.

'Do you know anyone capable of a set-up like this, Manuel?'

'I know some who'd quite like to put a bullet in you, but it'd never occur to them to involve you in a vice case.'

He cleared his throat and added:

'As for me, I'm no angel, but I swear to you, on Aline's life, that I had no idea about any of this before you came in. For the rest, we'll see . . .'

It was a surprise to hear Aline's voice again. She was no longer addressing Manuel. The timbre was no longer high-pitched and irritating, and the accent had almost disappeared.

'Maybe if you tell us the story, it might give me an idea. When a woman's in the picture, it's often better to ask another woman.'

The prefect with his new broom would probably have choked with indignation if he had known that a detective chief inspector, the head of the Crime Squad, was confiding in a former prostitute and a man who was thought, rightly or wrongly, to be an underworld boss.

In a few sentences, Maigret related his adventure. Aline didn't smile. As the story went on, there were more creases in her forehead, and she remained motionless on the edge of the divan, her legs still crossed, her chin in her hands.

'You don't have a photograph of her?'

'No.'

'And you haven't yet been to Boulevard de Courcelles to question her face to face?'

'I'm not allowed.'

'Well, my friend, she must be in a real fix!'

Maigret turned quickly towards her, struck by her exclamation.

'Why in a fix?'

'Put yourself in her shoes. Here's a rich girl from a good family, living with an uncle who's an important person and all that. She's never seen you. She probably only knows you because she's seen your name in the papers. And yet she puts on this act for you, an act that could go badly wrong. She gets home at eight in the morning, knowing that her uncle will be furious and is going to give her a grilling and try to catch her out. How old did you say she was?'

'Eighteen.'

'It's the right age. If you want my opinion, this girl is crazy about a man who can do anything he wants with her. He dictated to her what she had to say and put the whole plan together. Once you get your hands on him . . .'

She added with a hint of admiration:

'When girls like that put their minds to it, they can be bigger sluts than the real whores. What do you think, Daddy?'

'The same as you . . . I don't like this story.'

Once Maigret was in the lift, did they look at each other and laugh? Maigret would have sworn they didn't. They'd both seemed quite worried when he left.

For his part, he had learned nothing, and he didn't feel proud of himself as he looked for the bistro where his two inspectors were waiting for him. He found it immediately, next door to the mansion where the dentist had his surgery.

'A draught beer!'

He was thirsty. Never mind Pardon! He was starting to resent the doctor for their conversation the previous week. Pardon had advised him to take it easy, implying that he was gradually becoming an old man who would soon be good for nothing but fishing in the Loire. The prefect would have been delighted.

'I'm sorry, chief,' Lourtie stammered, his elbows on the bar. 'I couldn't have known the woman would—'

'It's all right.'

'Do you want me to stay?'

'Yes, until you're relieved. Let's go, Janvier.'

And a little later, as they drove:

'Go via Boulevard de Courcelles.'

He looked at the numbers. Number 42 was just opposite the main entrance to the Parc Monceau, its gates adorned with golden arrows. Children could be heard yelling, under the watchful eyes of an attendant in a blue uniform. The building was huge. The carriage entrance was enormous and very high, with a man posted on each side, and you could imagine the carriages with their frisky horses entering the courtyard, where the stables had been turned into garages.

Fortress. That was what Maigret called such buildings in his own mind. It wasn't a concierge who was in charge of the lodge but a figure in livery, and you certainly wouldn't smell stew simmering in a pot. The staircase was probably of marble, the apartments vast with high ceilings, covered in carpets that muffled the sound of footsteps.

These apartment buildings in the smarter neighbourhoods had made a great impression on him when he had first arrived in Paris. The valets still wore striped waistcoats, the maids lace caps, and the nurses, pushing prams in the park, English uniforms.

Quite often since then, he had had occasion to conduct investigations in these houses, and he had always felt the same embarrassment, and perhaps a certain aggressiveness – although not because of envy.

Experience had taught him that most of the inhabitants were somehow untouchable. If they weren't themselves influential figures, they had friends in high places and would threaten to complain, the way that Prieur had complained directly to the minister of the interior.

Janvier had slowed down. The car had almost stopped. Maigret muttered under his breath:

'The bitch!'

Then, in a resigned, bitter tone, aware of his own powerlessness:

'Let's go! Back to HQ.'

Quai des Orfèvres, where they could bombard anyone they liked with questions for twenty-four hours, or even for two or three days, with intervals for beer and sandwiches and short rests on a straw mattress. Anyone, but not these people, not Mademoiselle Nicole Prieur.

Janvier remained silent, understanding that now was not the time to open his mouth.

'A girl from her background almost certainly travels

abroad,' Maigret suddenly remarked. 'Which means she has a passport. There must be a file with her photograph at the Préfecture.'

He was very familiar with the office where these files were stored in green-painted metal cabinets. A hundred times he had turned to the official who kept them up to date, a man named Loriot, who never hesitated to open them for him.

But not when it came to Mademoiselle Prieur! He was obliged to go about it another way. Aline was right: he needed a photograph of the girl as soon as possible.

'Does Barnacle still have his Leica?'

'He'd give up his wife sooner than his camera.'

'He has a wife?'

It was odd: Maigret had known Inspector Barnacle for more than thirty years and yet had never known anything about his private life.

He had thought he was a bachelor. With his loose-fitting black suit, its sleeves frayed and its elbows shiny with use, which he'd been wearing for years and which was always missing a button, with his air of someone who is crushed beneath the burden of misfortune, Barnacle was more like a man recently widowed, whose grief hasn't yet had time to fade.

He had been at the Police Judiciaire when Maigret had first arrived. Maigret had called him monsieur and he still did. The result was that the inspectors also said Monsieur Barnacle, with a touch of irony, as if 'monsieur' were a name or a nickname.

Back in his office, he rang for the old clerk.

'Send me Monsieur Barnacle, if he's around.'

There was less bustle now in the offices and corridors. It was nearly six o'clock. The sun was still high, and there was no wind yet. The curtains on either side of the windows hung straight, without a quiver.

'You sent for me, sir?'

'Take a seat, Monsieur Barnacle.'

The inspector was only two and a half years older than him. In two and a half years' time, would Maigret also have that resigned expression, those eyes devoid of joy or curiosity, that worn, flabby skin, those weary shoulders?

Had Barnacle ever been different? He was married. Which meant he had once been more or less in love. He had courted a girl, bought her violets, walked arm in arm with her, stopped to kiss her. It was almost inconceivable.

'Not only is he married,' Janvier had just informed him, 'but they say locally that his wife is still generous with her favours. She often comes home late, sometimes stays out all night, and he's the one who makes dinner and does the housework when he gets back from work.'

Barnacle was certainly no great brain, but once he was on the trail of something, he didn't let go. In a crowd, he could be as inconspicuous as those grey walls covered in half-torn posters you saw in Paris.

'I'd like to entrust you with an assignment, Monsieur Barnacle, and the only reason I'm hesitating is that if anyone higher up hears about it, you might be forced into early retirement.'

'That would just mean three fewer months tramping the streets.'

There was no reproach in his voice. Barnacle wasn't an

embittered man, he bore nobody a grudge; probably he didn't bear his wife a grudge either.

'I'll carry out your assignment, sir.'

'There's a girl I want you to photograph. Where, when or how, I don't know, that's up to you.'

'I'm used to it.'

It was true. They often called on Barnacle's talents as a photographer as well as his shabby appearance. Whenever they needed a photograph of a suspect, he would position himself in a place where the suspect was almost certain to pass and, with his Leica on his chest, would pretend to be one of those street photographers you saw increasingly often on the Champs-Élysées, the Grands Boulevards and pretty much all over Paris.

He had even had printed, like them, little cards with a fictitious name and address and a number, which he would hand out to people.

'She lives on Boulevard de Courcelles and studies at the Sorbonne. She has a friend on Boulevard Saint-Germain, the daughter of Dr Bouet. You'll find his number in the phone book. Apart from that, I don't know who she sees or where she spends her days.'

'Does she own a car?'

'If she does, she hasn't had it long, because she's only eighteen. Her uncle is an important person, Master of Requests at the Council of State, and I assume he has a car and a chauffeur . . . I warn you, if you try the concierge, he'll immediately inform the prefect's office. And the prefect has expressly forbidden us from bothering her. You get the picture?'

'It may take a bit more time. Can you tell me what she looks like?'

Maigret gave him a description of Nicole Prieur.

'In this weather,' Monsieur Barnacle said as if to himself, 'it's quite likely she doesn't spend the afternoon at home. These people dine late. I may still have time.'

At the door, he turned with what might pass for a smile on his grey face.

'But if I get into trouble, don't do anything for me. I've been waiting for so long to tell them to piss off!'

Maigret couldn't get over it. Barnacle had always been so meek and mild, and now, three months from his retirement, he had revealed himself to be seething with anger. He added with a sneer:

'They don't have the right to touch my pension. They owe it to me, you understand? It's my money, money they've held back from me all these damned years.'

Maigret signed some papers that had been left on his desk. There was nothing else he could do without the photograph. He felt empty, useless.

All the same, he opened the door to the inspectors' room, out of habit, as he did every evening before leaving the Police Judiciaire. Lucas was there, his head a lot balder than when he had first joined Maigret's team.

'Come here a moment.'

He was upset at not being able to keep him informed. It wasn't because of the prefect's orders – after all, he'd spoken to Janvier – but because he couldn't bring himself to tell that humiliating story yet again.

'Come in. Sit down if you want.'

'Is everything all right, chief?'

'Not really, no. It doesn't matter. You don't by any chance know anyone studying at the Sorbonne, do you?'

'What subject?'

'No idea.'

'You know there are thousands of students.'

Lucas was looking down at the carpet, apparently thinking it over.

'I do know one of the porters, who's some kind of relative of my wife, but he's only a porter.'

'Are the two of you on good terms?'

'I meet him every three or four years when there's a family get-together, a funeral or a wedding . . .'

'Could you phone him and arrange to meet him somewhere? In a café, for example?'

'I'll see if he's on duty.'

'Phone from here.'

The man who was more or less a cousin of Madame Lucas was named Oscar Coutant, and they finally got him on the line.

'Lucas, yes . . . How are you? . . . No, she's fine . . . She asked me to say hello from her . . . Aunt Emma? We haven't seen her for at least three months . . . As deaf as ever, yes . . . Listen, I need some information, could we meet? . . . No, nothing important . . . I'd rather not come there . . . What? . . . Six thirty? . . . I just have time to get there . . . First on the left, coming from Boulevard Saint-Michel? . . . I'll be there.'

Lucas threw Maigret a questioning glance.

'All right. See you later.'

And, to Maigret:

'We got him just as he was about to leave. He'll wait for us in a bar in Rue Monsieur-le-Prince, where he usually stops for an aperitif on his way home. What should I ask him?'

'It's best if I go with you. Call a taxi, now.'

Apart from a little white wine with meals . . . Pardon had decreed.

How many bars had Maigret been obliged to enter in the past twenty-four hours? Of course, he could have ordered fruit juice . . .

At the age of forty, Oscar Coutant had the flabbiness of those men who sit still all day long and are partial to aperitifs. He was clearly proud of his position, which he probably kept up in a dignified, even solemn manner. He worked at the Sorbonne, shook hands with illustrious professors as they passed, didn't hesitate to reprimand, when need be, students who bore well-known names and would one day be bankers or ministers.

'Let me introduce my boss, Detective Chief Inspector Maigret.'

'Pleased to meet you. I've never seen you at our place.'

He was clearly not talking about his apartment, but about the Sorbonne.

'I'm glad to be able to help, inspector. It's always nice to meet famous people. And they don't come more famous than you! I always pictured you heavier, if you don't mind me saying so. Heavier and taller. We must be the same height, and I weigh eighty . . . What'll you have? A little anisette? Jules! Same again for me and two anisettes for these gentlemen . . . So, are you interested in one of our kids?'

'I wonder if you know a student named Nicole Prieur.'

'The niece of the—'

'Yes.'

'She's in the Étoile gang. They make life difficult for us, those kids, you have to be firm with them. There are about twenty of them, boys and girls. They drive up in these big sports cars, Jaguars, Ferraris, whatever, and park them in the spots reserved for the professors. Luckily, not all the teachers have cars, most of them use the Métro.'

'What is she studying?'

'Wait, let me picture the board. We keep all that up to date, you understand, but there are so many names to remember.'

Listening to him, you would have thought he carried the whole weight of the Sorbonne on his shoulders.

'Ah, yes, I remember now. She's doing art history, along with a friend of hers, the daughter of a doctor named Bouet.'

'Who else belongs to this Étoile gang?'

'We call it that because most of them live near the Arc de Triomphe: Avenue Hoche, Avenue Marceau, Avenue Foch and so on. The craziest is the son of a South American ambassador, who drives a blue Ferrari convertible. His name's Martinez, and there are always lots of girls with him. Another one, a tall fair-haired fellow, is the son of Dariman, who makes the chemical products. You know, the gang isn't always the same. They quarrel. You see new ones. They spend the evening and most of the night together in a club.'

'Do you know where?'

'It's been mentioned in the newspapers. Of course, I don't go to places like that myself, so I'm not really up to date. It's on Avenue de la Grande-Armée or somewhere round there. There's a restaurant on the ground floor, anyone can eat there, if they can afford it. The club's in the basement, and for that you apparently have to be a member . . . Wait, I'm trying to remember the name . . . It's on the tip of my tongue . . .'

'The Hundred Keys?' Lucas suggested.

'That's the one. How did you know?'

'Because, like you, I read about it in the papers. Once you're accepted as a member, you're given a gold key, which is like a symbol to say that you can open the doors of the club.'

Maigret stood up as the cousin was getting ready to order another round and launch into interminable reflections on the Sorbonne.

'I'm very grateful to you. I hope you don't mind, but I have to go.'

A little later, on Boulevard Saint-Michel, he collapsed on to the back seat of a taxi and said:

'Boulevard Richard-Lenoir.'

'Got it, Monsieur Maigret.'

It wouldn't be long before the prefect of police banned taxi drivers from recognizing him!

He had seldom been so eager to get back home and see his wife's bright, tender eyes.

5.

As soon as she recognized his steps on the stairs, she came and opened the door to him. She was in her housecoat and slippers, and the apartment smelled of floor polish.

'Sorry I'm not dressed, but when you asked them to call and tell me that you wouldn't be back for lunch, I assumed you were on a new case and I took the opportunity to wax the floor. What's the matter? Is something worrying you?'

'I am on a new case, as you put it. The Maigret case.'

He gave a forced smile. It is painful, towards the end of a career like his, to see your chiefs begin to doubt you, especially a proud, fiercely ambitious young cock of the walk like the prefect.

The morning's indignation might have faded, but there was still a residue of bitterness, which Maigret had made an effort not to show his colleagues, particularly his good old Janvier and Lucas.

'We may be in Meung-sur-Loire earlier than planned.'

'What are you talking about?'

'That business from last night. The phone call, the girl I went to see in Rue de Seine.'

'Don't tell me she was dead when you got there?'

'From my point of view, it's almost worse. She went home at eight in the morning. She lives on Boulevard de Courcelles, and her uncle is an important political figure.'

'It's funny. I've been thinking all day about that girl and what she told you. Something's been bothering me.'

'She's accused me of approaching her in a bar where she'd stopped to phone a friend and trying to get round her by promising to let her watch me arrest someone. Taking advantage of her innocence, I supposedly got her drunk, dragged her from one bar to another and eventually, when she was barely conscious, took her to a hotel room and undressed her against her will.'

'And people have believed that?'

'Lots of important people, apparently, starting with the minister of the interior, and continuing with the prefect of police.'

'Have you offered to resign?'

'Not yet.'

'You're going to defend yourself, I hope?'

'I've been trying to since eleven this morning. That's one of the reasons I'm asking you out to dinner.'

'Perfect timing. As I had no idea what time you were coming home, there are only cold cuts for dinner. What would you like me to put on?'

'The best you've got.'

A few minutes later, in the shower, he tried to hear what his wife was saying to him. They were forced to speak very loudly.

'Did you question the girl?'

'I'm forbidden to go anywhere near her or her place of residence.'

'Why did she do it? Do you have any idea?'

'Not yet. I may get one this evening.'

They dressed, exchanging words full of trust. Madame Maigret hadn't panicked, and she had been the first to mention the word 'resignation'. Not for a moment had she doubted her husband, and she had lost none of her good humour.

'Where are we going?'

'To a restaurant on Avenue de la Grande-Armée that has two stars in the Michelin guide.'

These were the longest days of the year. The sun hadn't yet set, and the whole of Paris had flung open its windows to the cooling air of evening. Men in shirt-sleeves were smoking their pipes or cigarettes and watching the passers-by, women in night attire were calling to one another from window to window, and as you walked along the street you could hear the cacophony of radios tuned to different stations.

They went down into the Métro. Some of his colleagues teased Maigret about this. He was one of the few at Quai des Orfèvres not to own a car. That was partly due to the fact that, when he'd been of an age to learn to drive and to enjoy it, he hadn't had the wherewithal.

It was too late now. There was a risk that when he was at the wheel, he would spend his time gazing up at the sun playing in the foliage of the trees, turning to look at a passer-by or else, when he was on a case, drifting off in sullen speculation.

He thought about this ironically as he sat beside his wife in the Métro carriage, swaying backwards and forwards and from side to side like her and the other passengers.

Madame Maigret could have driven him around. Many men let their wives do the driving.

'Can you see me responsible for a ton of scrap metal speeding away at a hundred kilometres an hour? I'd be so afraid of hurting someone! Especially as the traffic police are always urging you to go faster.'

Janvier had a 6CV. Lucas was talking of buying one. Maigret would be obliged to use a car when he lived in Meung-sur-Loire, unless he and his wife led the life of a provincial couple from the year 1900. In the country, he might get used to it and not be afraid of mistaking red lights for children's balloons. He'd still come to Paris by train as he used to.

'What are you thinking about?'

'Nothing.'

Nothing and everything: life, his career, that morning's interview in the prefect's office, Manuel in his wheelchair, that strange girl Aline.

The restaurant, with discreet tulle curtains at the windows, was almost at the end of the avenue. It was cosy and elegant, but half empty at the moment, given that a good many of its regular customers were already in the country or by the sea. To the right of the main door, a staircase led down to the basement, where a large red curtain was drawn across the entrance.

'Would you like a table near one of the windows?'

'No, here.'

Maigret indicated one facing the stairs and stood aside to let his wife take her seat on the banquette. He studied the menu.

'Would you like duck à l'orange?'

'What else is there?'

'A whole page . . .'

They finally chose a refreshing vichyssoise and the duck, which was the dish of the day. The head waiter had joined the rest of his staff and was probably whispering to them:

'That's Detective Chief Inspector Maigret.'

They were all looking at him curiously. He was used to it, but despite what the prefect said, it wasn't a pleasant sensation.

'Did you have a particular reason for choosing this restaurant? We've never been here before.'

'I came here once a long time ago, while I was on some case or other. Unless I'm mistaken, I was on the trail of an international con man who often had lunch here.'

'It seems like a respectable place.'

'International con men only eat in respectable places and stay at the best hotels.'

It was nine o'clock. A young woman came in and headed down the stairs. She didn't look like a customer, more like a cloakroom girl or lavatory attendant.

Ten minutes later, it was the turn of a weary-looking man. He wasn't one of the gilded youth either, but was on the other side of the fence, the side of those who serve.

The club downstairs probably opened later and they were now getting things ready, the way they did in the morning in little bars and cafés.

They heard a burst of music, muffled by the red curtain, followed by others, all different: records were being tried out to check the sound level.

'Do you think it's better than mine?'

'No. Nothing here is better than at home.'

She was talking about the duck. They chatted about this and that. From time to time, when she sensed he wasn't looking at her, Madame Maigret looked gravely at her husband, trying to figure out how affected he was. He had ordered a vintage Saint-Émilion, but barely touched it.

Was she, too, wondering if he wasn't drinking too much and if that didn't have a good deal to do with his tiredness? Because he did seem tired. She and Pardon had had brief, surreptitious conversations about it, Maigret knew that. What had the doctor told her?

'How about cheese? I can see a very tempting brie . . .'

'I may have a small piece.'

Maigret turned to the head waiter. 'Tell me something. The club downstairs . . .'

'Yes, monsieur. The Hundred Keys.'

'Why a hundred?'

'That's not my responsibility. I deal with the restaurant, not the club.'

'Can anyone be admitted?'

'No. It's strictly private. You have to be a member.'

'How does one join?'

'Why, are you interested?'

He seemed amazed, and looked in turn at Maigret and Madame Maigret, who blushed.

'Does that surprise you?'

'No . . . Yes . . . It's mainly a club for young people, who come there to dance. They'll be here soon. Would you like me to call the master of ceremonies?'

He was already on his way down to the basement. He

stayed there for quite a long time, re-emerging in the company of a young man in a dinner jacket whom Maigret thought he recognized.

'This is Monsieur Landry. He can provide you with all the information you need.'

Landry held out his hand.

'Good evening, detective chief inspector.' He bowed to Madame Maigret. 'I'm honoured, madame. Not many people in Paris have been lucky enough to meet you, as your husband doesn't like to show you in public. Would you allow me?'

He grabbed a chair by its back, sat down on it and took a silver cigarette case from his pocket.

'I hope you don't mind if I smoke?'

He was about thirty-five. His dinner jacket was perfectly cut, and he wore it with the ease of someone who dresses up every evening.

He was a handsome man who might perhaps be criticized for being too sure of himself. There was something sardonic, even aggressive, in his eyes. His smile was charming, seductive even, but you sensed that at the slightest threat he would show his claws.

'I hear you're interested in our club?'

'I'm tempted to join. Unless there's an age limit?'

'We considered it at the start. We thought thirty, which would have kept out some excellent people. So you've heard of the Hundred Keys, Monsieur Maigret?'

'In a vague kind of way, and I'm rather surprised to find you here. You're the master of ceremonies, I understand?'

'Secretary, master of ceremonies, a bit of everything,

really. It's fashionable to use the term "master of ceremonies".'

Maigret had met Landry when he was not much more than eighteen and had just arrived from the provinces. His father was director of postal services in Angers or Tours, one of those big towns on the banks of the Loire anyway. Anxious to make his career in Paris, he had written gossip items for the newspapers, skilfully worming his way through the crowds at receptions and cocktail parties and approaching well-known people.

One day, he had come to see Maigret at Quai des Orfèvres, oozing self-confidence and displaying a press card from a weekly paper specializing in sensational revelations.

Marcel Landry had no doubts about anything, especially not himself.

'You understand, detective chief inspector, our readers aren't interested in the workings of the Police Judiciaire – the daily papers have talked a lot about them – they're interested in what happens behind the scenes. After all, if I can put it this way, all the dirty linen of Paris ends up here. I hope that expression doesn't shock you. Obviously I'm not talking about naming names. And I think I can say that my paper would be prepared to pay a good deal of money . . .'

He was too young at the time for Maigret to be angry with him, and he had quite gently shown him the door. Two or three years later, he had heard his voice on the radio, presenting commercials.

Then there had been a gap. Landry was one of those characters you meet everywhere for a while, so that you grow used to shaking their hands without knowing exactly who they are, and who then disappear suddenly, for no apparent reason, until they resurface in a different guise.

What obscure professions had Landry practised during those years? If he had broken the law, it hadn't reached the ears of the police. For a time he had been the secretary – and escort – to a female singing star.

On leaving her two or three years later, he wrote a memoir revealing the smallest details of the star's private life, and she took him to court.

Maigret had no idea if she had won or lost the case, but now here he was again, simultaneously cheerful and nervous, sixteen or seventeen years older than the young man he had known, but still looking remarkably well-preserved.

'The thing is, the Hundred Keys isn't like all the other clubs that open every week in Paris. It's a real club. You genuinely have to be a member to get through the red curtain downstairs. As for the figure of a hundred, it's there to limit the number of members. Actually, to date, there are only eighty-five or eighty-six.'

'Young men and women from well-to-do families, I assume?'

'To make it more exclusive, we fixed the subscription at six hundred francs. The drinks, on the other hand, are only a little above cost price. Do you dance?'

Maigret was so surprised that he didn't immediately grasp the meaning of the question.

'Pardon me?'

'I asked you if you like to dance. Modern dances, obviously – we don't expect anyone here to dance the waltz or the polka. Do you also dance, Madame Maigret?'

Not knowing what to reply, she looked to her husband for help.

'Yes, we both dance! Does that surprise you?'

'A little. I've never seen you on a dance floor, and given your reputation . . .'

'A clumsy oaf sucking grumpily at his pipe.'

'I didn't say that. Do you really want to join?'

'Yes, I do.'

'Do you know two members of the club who could be your sponsors? That's another thing that shows this is a real club. Any candidate has to be proposed by two sponsors, and the application is submitted to a committee of twelve members, who have to come to a majority decision.'

'If I could have a look at the list of members, I'm sure I'd find more than two people of my acquaintance who'd support my application.'

Marcel Landry didn't bat an eyelid. They both knew they were playing a game. Landry gave Maigret a sharp look, intrigued rather than anxious, recovered his smile and walked to the stairs. When he returned, he was holding a register bound in red leather.

'This book is always kept at the members' disposal on a pedestal table behind the curtain. As you can see, it contains not only the names and addresses of the subscribers but also those of everyone's sponsors. I'd be surprised if you found any of your clients here . . . Look, under *A*: Abouchère, the son of Senator Abouchère . . . The Vicomte d'Arceau. He doesn't use his title when he comes here. His father's a member of the Jockey Club and he'll be a member one day, just like his grandfather and his grandfather's father . . . Barillard, from the Barillard Oils people. Next month, Mademoiselle Barillard is marrying Eric Cornal – Cornal Biscuits, you know. She met him here . . . You could say this register is something like a young people's *Who's Who*. Some of them are students, and we don't see much of them at this time of year, because the exams are on. Others have jobs. We also have couples . . .'

All of the addresses were what might be called good addresses, the kind that place people in a specific social category.

Maigret moved his lips as he ran his index finger down the page, stopping at a name.

François Mélan, 38, specialist in oral medicine: 32a, Rue des Acacias.

'Isn't he the dentist who has a clinic in a small mansion?'

'I confess I've never been there. He comes here often, although he doesn't dance much. Apparently, he's a remarkably intelligent man.'

The finger descended and stopped again, Maigret making an effort not to show his interest.

Nicole Prieur, 17: 42, Boulevard de Courcelles.

The most interesting thing was further on, in the sponsors' column. Those for Nicole were none other than Dr François Mélan and Martine Bouet.

'Isn't Mademoiselle Bouet a tall blonde?'

'I see you know her. She's one of the best dancers in the club. Great friends with Mademoiselle Prieur.'

'Does Mademoiselle Prieur come here often?'

Landry drummed nervously on the table with his fingers. He might not have had anything to feel guilty about, but in the uncertain career he had chosen, and given his ambitions, it wasn't a sensible idea to antagonize the police.

The prefect's instructions hadn't yet reached Avenue de la Grande-Armée. Madame Maigret, for her part, sat watching her husband at work with great curiosity. This was the first time she'd had the opportunity, and she was trying her best to guess what lay behind the apparently trivial dialogue the two men were conducting.

'Mademoiselle Prieur is one of our most loyal members. She's here at least two or three times a week.'

'Alone?'

'Alone or in a group.'

'Does she stay until closing time?'

'Quite often.'

'What time do you close?'

'It depends on the atmosphere. Members sometimes bring with them a film star, a theatre star, a singer, some celebrity or other. There are nights when we don't turn the lights out until six in the morning, but mostly it's two or three, when there's nobody left.'

'Has Mademoiselle Prieur ever come with her uncle?'

'Once, at the beginning. For most of the younger girls, it's almost a tradition. The first night, the relatives like to see things for themselves. Monsieur Prieur surprised all of us. We were expecting to see somebody solemn . . . Do you know him?'

'No.'

'He's the Master of Requests at the Council of State, and they say he's one of our most learned jurists. Well, just imagine a man of fifty or fifty-five with broad shoulders, a square-cut face like a peasant's, a short thick beard covering his face, and bushy eyebrows. A good-natured boar. He ordered a double whisky, and less than a quarter of an hour later he was on the dance floor with his niece. He stayed for two hours and when he left he congratulated me, adding that if he wasn't such an early riser, he'd have stayed even longer.'

'It's easy to get the wrong idea about people. Did he ever come back?'

'No.'

'Not even last night?'

'Definitely not.'

'Who was Mademoiselle Prieur with last night?'

'Last night? Wait, I have to picture the layout of tables in my mind . . . No, I didn't see her last night.'

'Or her friend?'

'You mean Martine Bouet? . . . No. I can't place her either.'

'Many thanks.'

'Do you still want to apply for membership? Have you found any possible sponsors on this list?'

'Lots of them. I'll think about it. I see your members are starting to arrive.'

'Actually, yes, it's time I went down.'

'By the way, do you know Manuel?'

'The actor?'

'Manuel Palmari.'

'What does he do?'

'Nothing.'

'I don't think so . . . No . . . Should I know him?'

'It's better you don't. Thanks again, Monsieur Landry.'

'Wouldn't you like to take a look downstairs? Or you, madame? . . . In that case, if you'll excuse me . . .'

Madame Maigret waited patiently until her husband had paid the bill and they were both outside before asking:

'Did you find out what you wanted?'

'I found out a lot of things, but I don't know how important they are. While we're in the area, let's go by Rue des Acacias.'

On the way, he sighed:

'As long as Nicole Prieur doesn't think of going to the club this evening.'

'Do you think he'll talk?'

'He's bound to tell her that I asked him a lot of questions about her. If she then tells her uncle, we can start packing our bags tomorrow.'

He said this in such a light tone that she squeezed his arm more tightly and asked:

'Are you sad? Are you trying to hide it from me?'

'No. To be honest, at the point I am now, I'm wondering which I'd rather do: leave or carry on.'

'I guess it was a big shock this morning?'

'Fairly. For the first time in my life, I was on the wrong side of the desk. I wonder if I'll still have the heart to go on with some of my interrogations.'

'Why didn't you defend yourself?'

'Because there would have been no point, and I might have lost my temper.'

'You think that girl—'

'She doesn't count. She's just a pawn. Everything's too well engineered, including the question of the times, the two possible testimonies . . . Martine Bouet, first of all. The telephone token. Just one . . . Then Désiré. She definitely wasn't unsteady on her feet when he saw her and didn't talk to him as if she was drunk. When she spoke to me, she lowered her voice, and he couldn't hear her . . . The bars where I'm supposed to have got her drunk. The description she gave could apply to fifty bars and cellars in Saint-Germain-des-Prés, and at least a dozen of those places are so crowded that nobody would have noticed us . . . And finally, the hotel. Well, I did go up to the second floor with her, and she was clever enough to keep me in her room for a good ten minutes . . .'

'Do you have any ideas?'

'Bits of ideas. Lots of bits. Unfortunately, only one of these bits is the right one. I just have to decide which it is.'

Rue des Acacias was almost deserted. There were still some lighted windows, including two of the windows in the dentist's house. Maigret went up to the nameplate, which he had only seen from a distance during his visit to Manuel:

Dr François Mélan, specialist in oral medicine.
10 a.m. to midday, then by appointment.

'Why does he put "specialist in oral medicine"?'

'It sounds posher than "dentist".'

He looked up at Manuel's window and saw Aline leaning there, smoking a cigarette.

A few metres further on, a man standing on a corner murmured as Maigret and his wife passed:

'Goodnight, sir.'

It was Jaquemain, one of his inspectors, who would be spending the night in the street.

'Goodnight, old man.'

The couple took the Métro at Ternes. It had been a depressing day, but thanks to Madame Maigret it was drawing to a close in comparative serenity. On Boulevard Richard-Lenoir, a big rose-tinted moon looked down on them as they walked arm in arm towards their apartment.

A traffic accident delayed the bus in which he was travelling, and he didn't get to Quai des Orfèvres until 9.10.

'Has anyone asked for me?'

'No, sir. Only Inspector Lourtie.'

'I'll see him after the briefing.'

He took the files that were on his desk and hurried to the commissioner's office, where the other department heads were already gathered.

'My apologies, commissioner.'

'You were saying, Bernard?'

The head of the Gambling Squad went on with his report, in a monotonous voice.

'Good . . . And what about you, Maigret? Another jewel raid yesterday . . .'

Maigret had expected a difficult session, furtive or reproving glances, but nothing of what had happened the previous day in the prefect's office seemed to have filtered through.

The usual morning routine. The open windows. Birds singing. A tramp on the banks of the Seine, carefully washing his linen.

A quarter of an hour later, Barnacle, still dressed in black, slipped into Maigret's office.

'I have three,' he announced, holding out some enlarged photographs, 'but I don't know which is the right one.'

He meant the right girl, in other words, Nicole Prieur. The first, a round-faced young woman with innocent eyes, looked nothing like her. The second was barely sixteen, which rather suggested that poor Barnacle's knowledge of girls had remained rudimentary.

The third was indeed Nicole, wearing a light-coloured dress and carrying a white handbag under her arm.

'I have another one of her, a full-length one.'

Like a conjurer, Barnacle produced it from a pocket of his loose-fitting jacket. The picture had been taken in front of the gates of the Parc Monceau. Nicole was holding on to a dog lead, at the other end of which a dachshund was busy doing its business.

'Is this what you wanted?'

'Perfect, Barnacle.'

'Would you like more copies?'

'If possible, yes. Three or four.'

It didn't matter so much now. Without Oscar, Lucas' – or rather, Madame Lucas' – distant relative, these photographs would have played a greater role. They might still play one, although Maigret already thought he had a lead.

'Do you want me to print them right away?'

Maigret had rather forgotten that Barnacle had risked his job to take these photographs on the sly.

'Was it difficult?'

'Not as difficult as all that. Out in the street, you know, I'm not conspicuous, I blend into the background. In parks, you almost always find one or two men like me, and nobody pays attention to them any more.'

He spoke of himself without bitterness or irony.

'She didn't notice a thing. She was busy with her dog. It wouldn't cross the road, and she had to pick it up and carry it. I have a picture of her holding the dog, but it's out of focus, and I didn't print it.'

'Thanks, Barnacle. You're a good man.'

'Well, you've always been good to me.'

Once Barnacle had left, it was Janvier's turn.

'Is this the girl?'

'Yes. I'd like you to go to Rue Fontaine.'

'The Clou Doré?'

'Yes. Show the picture to the waiters. Try and find out if they've ever seen her there. Then try the surrounding area.'

'Aren't you going out, chief?'

'Yes. I'm going to Rue des Acacias.'

'Don't you need me to drive you?'

'I'd prefer you to go to Montmartre before the rush starts. Tell Lucas to wait for me downstairs with a car.'

There was already a heat haze in the air, the kind you see over the sea, and the Champs-Élysées shimmered in a golden light.

'Thanks for the cousin, Lucas.'

'You're welcome, chief. Because of me, he has quite a hangover. He was so proud of meeting you and having a drink with you that he couldn't stop with the anisettes. From now on, he's going to talk about his friend Maigret as if he's known you since your schooldays. Where should I drop you? At Manuel's?'

It had already become a habit.

'If you like. I'm going to the house opposite.'

'Shall I wait for you?'

'Yes. I may not be long.'

He rang the doorbell. A woman with a long face, Spanish in appearance, looked at him in an unfriendly fashion and asked:

'What do you want?'

'I'd like to see Dr Mélan.'

'Do you have an appointment?'

'Yes.'

'Go up then. The door on the right.'

She watched him as he climbed the stairs. They were of oak and partly covered in a stained green carpet. The woman's apron was stained, too. Madame Maigret would have found the place poorly maintained.

6.

He took his time, just for the pleasure of making the maid hang about in the ground-floor corridor. And as he climbed the stairs, he tried to define the smell that pervaded the house, a smell he knew, one not without its charm, which went back as far as his childhood: the smell of old houses, damp woodwork, with a whiff of compost.

The little mansion probably still had a garden at the back, the kind you still found in Paris, with a tree which, again because of the smell, Maigret would have sworn was a lime tree.

He had never been in quite such a difficult position: he had no right to be here, and, if the dentist made even the smallest complaint, there would be an official disclaimer and Maigret would have to account for his actions.

It was as if he were deliberately doing all the things the prefect accused him of. No sooner had there been mention of his liking for informers than he had rushed to see Manuel, who was one.

He had been forbidden to talk to Nicole and he had gone and questioned an employee of the Sorbonne about her in a bar.

The slightest mention of this case at the Police Judiciaire was forbidden, and he had informed first Janvier, then Lucas, and sent poor Barnacle to secretly photograph the girl.

Finally, on a pretext so transparent that Marcel Landry hadn't been taken in for a moment, he had asked to see the register of a private club of which Monsieur Prieur's niece was a member.

All these offences in just one day! Having ventured this far, he saw no reason to stop. Either he would succeed or he would fail, and as far as everyone was concerned his career would come to a pitiful end.

Had he even discovered anything? Yes. He wasn't yet sure how valuable the information was, but he had found a connection between two women as different, living such diametrically opposed lives, as Nicole Prieur and Manuel's mistress, Aline. Nicole had had Dr Mélan as her sponsor for the Hundred Keys. At least once, the previous day, Aline had gone to the same dentist for treatment.

All this went through his head in a few seconds. When he got to the first floor, he turned, not to the door on the right, as the Spanish woman had told him, but the one on the left. He quite liked to see the private surroundings of the people he was dealing with, especially rooms he hadn't been invited into.

The door was locked or bolted. A voice from below said: 'Don't you know your right from your left?'

The maid had walked up a few steps. Her big dark eyes had not much more expression than those of a cow in a meadow, but she was a fine figure of a woman all the same.

An enamel plaque bore the words: *Knock and come in.*

He knocked, turned the handle and found himself in a waiting room that looked like a sitting room in the provinces, empty apart from one other person, a still fairly young woman, clearly anxious and in poor health.

Ignoring the pile of magazines on a gilded pedestal table, she sat there motionless, staring down at the flowered carpet. She cast him a brief, indifferent glance, then went back to her melancholy contemplation.

A door opposite him opened, and the long-nosed secretary or nurse Manuel had told him about addressed him in an unfriendly manner. Her voice was curt, her gaze harsh. She was the kind of exceptionally ugly woman who has never had a childhood or an adolescence and blames the whole world for it.

'What is it you want?'

'I'd like to see Dr Mélan.'

'For a consultation?'

'Yes.'

'Do you have an appointment?'

'No.'

'The doctor only sees patients by appointment.'

'The nameplate by the door says that he sees patients from ten to midday, and by appointment only after midday.'

'It's an old nameplate.'

'I've had a bad toothache since last night, and aspirin doesn't help. I'd like the doctor to—'

'Have you been here before?'

'No.'

'Do you live locally?'

'No.'

'What made you choose Dr Mélan?'

'I was passing in the street and saw his nameplate.'

'Follow me.'

She admitted him to a small office with white walls, although the white was as faded as in the rest of the building. She sat down at the desk.

'Take a seat. I can't guarantee the doctor will be able to fit you in between patients, but I'll fill in a file card for you just in case. What's your name?'

'Maigret. Jules Maigret.'

'Profession?'

'Civil servant.'

'Age?'

'Fifty-two.'

'Address?'

'Boulevard Richard-Lenoir.'

She didn't react. Admittedly, her head was bent over the form, and he couldn't see her eyes.

'Which is the tooth that hurts?'

'A molar on the right, I'm not sure which, the second one, I think . . .'

'Wait in the next room. I can't guarantee anything. If you're in a hurry, I advise you to find another dentist.'

'I'll wait.'

The window of the waiting room did indeed look out on a garden, and there, in the middle of a lawn that was wilting in the heat, he saw the lime tree he had imagined.

He also saw a dilapidated greenhouse up against quite a high wall, gardening tools, badly tended flowerbeds.

Beyond that was a building of six or seven floors. From this angle, it was the back of the building he saw. At several of the windows, clothes were drying on washing lines.

He sat down and fingered his pipe in his pocket. He might have lit it if that sad-looking young woman hadn't been sitting opposite him. There was a ticking. It came from a black marble clock just like those in the offices at Quai des Orfèvres. It showed the time to be 10.20. He wondered if he would still be here waiting when it showed twelve.

He made an effort not to think, to avoid constructing hypotheses, to keep his mind open, and to pass the time he registered small details: the mirror above the fireplace, where flies had left little brown marks over the years, the Second Empire andirons, the mismatched armchairs. Nothing was ugly in itself. Nor was the house, built in around 1870 or 1880, well before the apartment buildings in the street.

It would soon disappear. Its end was clearly near, which might have been why nobody could bother with the expense of a new coat of paint.

It was also obvious there was no wife here, no children.

The third door in the room was padded, the kind still found in old notaries' offices or in some government buildings. Nothing could be heard of whatever was happening beyond it.

In fact, there was silence throughout the building, and with the windows closed you could only just make out the singing of birds in the lime tree.

Outside, it was hot. Here, the coolness was striking.

'The doctor asks you to excuse him, mademoiselle. He'll see you in a few minutes.'

It was the nurse, to whom the young patient responded with a look of resignation.

'Please follow me, Monsieur Maigret.'

She opened the padded door, then the grey-painted door behind it, passing abruptly from shade to sunlight. A man in white was sitting at a Louis-Philippe desk, holding the file card recently filled out for Maigret.

The nurse had disappeared. François Mélan was taking his time, reading the card to the end. Maigret took two or three steps forwards.

'Take a seat.'

He was quite different from what might have been imagined from the conversation with Marcel Landry, and it was even harder to see him than Nicole's uncle in the music-filled basement of the Hundred Keys Club.

He was a genuine redhead, a flaming redhead, the kind whom, in their childhood, their schoolmates call Carrot Head. He looked up. Behind his thick glasses without visible frames was a pair of limpid blue eyes.

He seemed very young. At the age of thirty-eight, he might have been taken for a student.

'Did your toothache come on suddenly?'

He made no reference to Maigret's profession, and there was no curiosity in his gaze.

'Yes, last night, as I was going to bed.'

'Had it been hurting before? In the past few weeks?'

'No. I have quite good teeth. I haven't been to a dentist more than ten or so times in my life.'

'Let's have a look.'

He stood up, and Maigret made a new discovery: Mélan was huge, almost a head taller than him. His white coat, not much crisper than the nurse's, didn't cover his knees, and his trousers needed ironing.

The dentist's chair was in the middle of the room, and above it, as usual, was a round lamp, its bulb the colour of the full moon. Between the chair and the window was a narrow table with instruments laid out on it.

Maigret sat down gingerly. A little chain was put around his neck and a towel attached to it. Pressing on a pedal with his feet, Dr Mélan slowly raised the chair.

All this was commonplace. The same scene, with the same actions, was happening at this very moment in hundreds of Parisian dentists' surgeries.

'Put your head back . . . Good . . . Open your mouth.'

It wasn't quite as silent here as in the rest of the building. The surgery looked out on to the street. It didn't have frosted glass windows, but tulle curtains, through which it was possible to see the cream-coloured façade opposite, open windows, a woman coming and going in her kitchen.

The noises of the street were a vague murmur from which a few sharper sounds stood out.

Impassively, Mélan moved a little mirror over a flame and picked up a shiny instrument.

'Open wider, please.'

As he bent over, Maigret saw his face up close, as if through a magnifying glass. The skin was thick, reddish – as it is on many redheads – and grainy, with a few freckles.

Mélan didn't speak. Since Maigret had come in, he had uttered only a bare minimum of words and, when he stood up, unfolding his tall body, he had done so with the awkwardness of a shy person.

With the help of a sharp instrument, he scratched at the surface of the molars.

'Do you feel anything?'

'No,' Maigret tried to say, with his mouth open.

'What about now?'

'No.'

'Here?'

Still nothing. It was true. Maigret had almost never had any problems with his teeth. The dentist swapped his instrument for a little hammer.

'Am I hurting you?'

'It's not very pleasant.'

'But no sharp pain?'

Why, all at once, did Maigret vow that, whatever happened, he wouldn't allow himself to be injected? He was starting to be afraid. It wasn't panic, but a vague, indeterminate fear. There he was, almost lying down, his head back, his mouth open, somehow a prisoner in this chair.

Why had he come here? Because he was looking for the man who had mounted a spiteful attack on him. That was the word Pardon had used when he had asked him something like:

'In your career, have you ever encountered a truly wicked, spiteful criminal . . .'

He was looking for someone who, in order to get him out of the way, or from sheer hatred for him, had put all his efforts into disgracing him, constructing a complicated plan, putting it together meticulously, using as an instrument a young woman of good family. Actually, why did people say "a good family"? Because the others are from bad families?

He was here because he had his reasons, however vague, to suspect the red-haired dentist.

He couldn't read anything in the blue eyes magnified by the thick glasses. The features of the man's face were as stiff as concrete, and his breath smelled of stale cigarettes.

'Any man is capable of becoming a murderer if he has sufficient motive.'

Maigret had uttered these words once in answer to a question from Pardon or a journalist.

Now, someone had tried to disgrace him, to remove him overnight from his post.

Assuming it was Mélan . . . It hadn't even been twenty-four hours since the interview with the prefect of police and not only was Maigret still in his post, but he had actually come to the dentist's surgery . . .

This wasn't a reasoned argument, just vague thoughts, full of ifs and buts.

If Mélan – since it was in his surgery that Maigret was now – had sufficient motive to mount this plot, using Nicole as his instrument, didn't he also have sufficient motive to get rid of Maigret in another way?

'Rinse your mouth and spit.'

Maigret obeyed. Mélan watched him, standing there motionless, as impassive as ever.

'Your teeth are perfectly healthy and can't have been hurting you. If you were indisposed last night, if you really did feel stabbing pains on the right side of your jaw, it might be due to the onset of sinusitis.'

'Is there anything to be done about it?'

'That's up to your usual doctor.'

He turned his back to put away his instruments. Maigret extricated himself with some difficulty from the chair, which hadn't been lowered. Taking a step forwards, he found himself less than two metres from the window, and through the tulle curtains he spotted Aline, casually dressed, smoking a cigarette and looking out at the street.

He knew the layout of the rooms in the apartment opposite. The window where Aline was standing was the window of the little room where Manuel spent most of his day.

He turned slightly white, because this discovery instilled in him a retrospective fear, a fear that was much more specific than the one he had felt earlier.

'How much do I owe you?' he asked.

'You can settle that with my assistant.'

Still calm in appearance, still as awkward, his face unmoving, his eyes expressionless, Mélan opened the door to the small office where Maigret had been questioned for the file card.

Without a word, he closed the door again. The assistant pointed to the chair where Maigret had previously sat.

'Wait a moment.'

She was probably going to admit the sad-looking female patient.

On the desk was a long, narrow rack, in which the file cards were lined up in a block like decks of playing cards in a baccarat shoe. The temptation was a strong one. It might be a trap. Maigret didn't move.

'Do you have Social Security? If you could show me your card . . .'

He looked for it in his wallet, which was always stuffed full of pointless papers, and held it out to the woman, who noted the number.

'It's twenty francs for the consultation. Social Security will refund eighty per cent.'

She handed him back his card. She, too, made no attempt to be polite. She let him walk to the door and pressed a button that set off a faint ringing on the ground floor.

'You can go down.'

'Thank you.'

He was back on the staircase, with its smell. The Spanish woman was waiting for him at the foot of the stairs and followed him to the front door, which she closed behind him. Miraculously, Lucas had found a shady spot to park the car and was reading a newspaper behind the wheel.

Maigret looked up. He could no longer see Aline at her window. He walked over to the building opposite.

On the third floor, he rang the bell and heard the hum of a vacuum cleaner. He was greeted by the elderly cleaning woman he had seen during his previous visits.

'Are you here to see Monsieur Palmari?'

'And Mademoiselle Aline.'

'I think madame is in her bath. Come in anyway.'

He was back in the sitting room. The door to the little room was open, and Manuel was sitting there in his wheelchair, in silk pyjamas, listening to the radio. He turned it off reluctantly.

'Again?'

Maigret came forwards, and behind him the vacuum cleaner began humming again as it moved over the sitting-room carpet.

'It's actually Aline I'd like to speak to.'

'She was in here a few minutes ago.'

'I know. I saw her at the window.'

'She's gone to take a bath. What did you want with her?'

'To be honest, I'm not sure yet.'

'Listen, Monsieur Maigret. I've always been straight with you. I did you a few favours in the past, which if they'd been found out about at the time would have got me shot a lot earlier than three years ago. But now you're overdoing it. I'm fed up of being suspected of every job that's pulled in Paris. How would you feel if you were always being watched, always being asked pathetic questions, without even knowing why?'

'That pretty much applies to me right now, doesn't it?'

'All the more reason not to bother other people. Aline saw you earlier, getting out of a car and ringing the dentist's bell. All because she told you yesterday that she went to have her teeth seen to.'

'That wasn't the reason.'

'Then what was? I just don't get it any more. You're not going to tell me he's your dentist, too.'

'I'll wait for Aline. That way, I won't have to repeat myself.'

He walked over to the window and stood there with his hands in his pockets, looking particularly at the window opposite with the tulle curtains, behind which Dr Mélan was treating his patient.

Nothing could be seen inside. It was just about possible to make out some lighter patches, especially the dentist's white coat whenever he moved close to the window to pick up an instrument.

'How many times have I been here in a week, Manuel?'

'Three times. You take up so much room, I could quite easily say ten. When I was in Rue Fontaine, it didn't matter so much. In a bar, people come and go. Everyone's entitled to have a drink, and a lot of customers like to make conversation. Too bad for the owner if he gets disturbed. That's his job. But this is our apartment, Aline's and mine. A person's apartment is sacred, isn't it? Even the police can't come in without a warrant. Am I right?'

Maigret hadn't been listening and responded with a vague gesture.

'How many times while I was talking to you,' he asked, 'did I come and stand by this window?'

Manuel shrugged. The question struck him as idiotic.

'What I do know is that you don't stay seated for very long.'

Both in his office and in his apartment on Boulevard Richard-Lenoir, Maigret was in the habit of walking to the window and standing next to it, looking at whatever was there, the windows opposite, the trees, the Seine, passersby. Was it a sign of claustrophobia, perhaps? Wherever he was, he instinctively sought contact with the outside world.

Aline came in, wearing a canary-yellow bathrobe, droplets of water in her tousled hair.

'What was I saying yesterday? Has he brought his pyjamas?'

But seeing that Maigret looked more solemn than usual, she stopped joking.

'Listen, Aline, I'm not here to bother you, and I give you my word that the investigation I'm conducting has nothing to do with you or Manuel, at least not as far as I know.'

She was looking at him askance, still suspicious.

'Answer me honestly. It'll be better for everyone, believe me. Was yesterday the first time you'd ever been into the house opposite?'

'Definitely. It was the first time in my life I had toothache.'

'I saw you earlier, leaning at this window and smoking a cigarette.'

'You were there?'

She pointed to the window with the tulle curtains.

'In the same chair you'd been in. I suppose you spend a lot of time at the window?'

'Like anyone. You have to get a bit of air.'

'Do you know any of the residents of that house?'

'Are there many? I thought . . .'

'You thought what?'

'That there was only the dentist, Carola and the assistant.'

'Is Carola the maid?'

'Maid, cook, concierge, whatever. She runs the whole place herself. I sometimes run into her in the local shops. Because of her accent, I asked her if she was Spanish and she said yes. She's not very talkative, but we do say hello to each other.'

'What about the assistant?'

'Mademoiselle Motte.'

'Did Carola tell you her name?'

'Yes. She doesn't sleep in the house. At midday, she goes out for lunch in a little restaurant at the end of the street and comes back at about two. In the evening, she's not so regular. Sometimes she stays until seven or eight.'

'Do you know where she lives?'

'I've never wondered. She's even scarier up close than she is from a distance.'

'Did she fill out a file card for you?'

'Yes, like I was applying for a passport.'

'Did she ask you any indiscreet questions?'

'She asked me who'd given me the dentist's address. I told her I lived opposite. Actually, yes, she did ask me a strange question: "Which floor?"'

'Is that all?'

Aline thought about this. 'Pretty much . . . I can't think of . . . Wait, I was standing in front of her. She looked me up and down with her hard, nasty little eyes and asked: "Do you have any other health problems?" I told her I didn't and she didn't insist. You don't take a vaccination certificate with you when you go to the dentist's, do you?'

Manuel knew Maigret well enough to realize that he was edging closer to a still elusive truth. You could sense that he was sniffing in all directions, left and right . . . He showed Aline the photograph of Nicole Prieur.

'Did you ever see her in Rue Fontaine?'

'Is this the girl you mentioned yesterday?'

He nodded.

'Not in Rue Fontaine. But I have seen her in this street, on the pavement opposite.'

'Was she going to the dentist's?'

'That's right. Except that it wasn't during his usual consulting hours.'

'Late at night?'

'Not especially late. Nine, nine thirty.'

'Was the light on in the surgery?'

'Not those days.'

'You mean it is on other evenings?'

'Quite often, yes.'

'Can you see through the tulle curtains?'

'No. The shutters are closed. All the same you can see the light through the slats.'

'If I understand correctly, Nicole Prieur doesn't visit Dr Mélan as a patient.'

This was something he had known since the previous evening.

'Does the doctor see other people outside his consulting hours? Men? Women?'

Aline's eyes opened wide. 'Come to think of it, every now and again I do see people going in during the day, more women than men.'

'Young?'

'Some are young, some not so young. You know, I'm not a concierge, I don't spend my time spying on people's comings and goings. It just so happens I'm often at the window.'

'I'm always telling her off about it,' Manuel muttered. 'I've been wondering if she has a secret lover, or maybe she's just starting to get bored with me.'

'You're just stupid!'

'Stupid or not, I know how old I am, and this damned leg doesn't make things any better.'

'There aren't many young man who can touch you.'

The reference was clear, and Manuel beamed with pride. These two really did seem to love each other.

'In the evening, is it men, too?'

'What are you thinking?'

'Nothing specific yet. I'm groping my way.'

'Seems to me you're groping in some strange places.'

'What do you mean?'

'About these women in the evening. You think they're coming for something other than getting their teeth seen to, don't you? And since he sees them in his surgery, it's not to have sex either. There must be more comfortable places for that kind of thing in the house, and the dentist doesn't have a jealous wife to make a scene. So you're thinking they have something else that needs tending, not their mouths.'

'Have you ever been pregnant?'

She looked at Manuel, who shrugged.

'Like any other woman!'

'But you don't have children?'

'Don't even think about it! . . . It's a funny old world . . . When you don't want it, your belly gets big just from looking at a man . . . Then when, like now, you'd like to have a kid in the house – isn't that right, Daddy? – not a chance. And there's nothing you can do about it.'

'Was it a doctor who helped you?'

'In those days, I couldn't have afforded a medic. The ones who do that kind of thing ask for a ridiculous amount of money, because of the risk. So I went to see a lavatory attendant.'

'A lavatory attendant?'

'Don't tell me you don't know about it. There are at least ten of them in Montmartre, always ready to help young girls out of a jam for not too much.'

Her eyes were staring into space; she was remembering something.

'Hold on! If you're right, I understand now why the old bitch looked me up and down as if she was studying my anatomy. It also explains why she asked me if I had any other health problems apart from my teeth.'

'Did the dentist say anything unusual to you?'

'He hardly opened his mouth. From close up, you'd think his eyes were going to come out of that orange head of his. "Open your mouth . . . Rinse . . . Spit . . . Open . . ."'

'Are you supposed to be seeing him again?'

'Tomorrow morning. He put on a temporary dressing that's given me a nasty taste in my mouth. Even cigarettes taste horrible.'

'If I asked you—'

Here, Manuel intervened.

'Oh, no, Monsieur Maigret! We do you some little favours, all right. Which doesn't stop you trying to frame me, by the way. No, don't argue. I know what I'm talking about. But this business is like Aline's dressing: it stinks! So let me have my say. The answer is no! I won't even let her go back into that house. Dressing or no dressing, she'll just have to find another dentist.'

7.

At 11.30, Maigret walked into his office and flung his hat on an armchair. He didn't have time to choose a fresh pipe before there was a knock at the door, and old Joseph came in.

'The commissioner is asking to see you, sir. This is the third time he's sent me.'

As it happened, poor Barnacle with his sore feet wasn't the oldest in the Police Judiciaire, it was this clerk with his silver chain, who, thanks to spending most of his time in an antechamber where no daylight penetrated, had taken on the colour of ivory.

Maigret followed him and for the second time this morning entered the commissioner's office, whose threshold he had crossed thousands of times.

'Sit down, Maigret.'

He pointed to an armchair that was half in shade, half in sunlight. The three windows let all the noises from outside into the room, and the commissioner, as if to give this interview a more confidential character, stood up and closed them.

He appeared more than embarrassed. His name was Roland Blutet. Ever since his appointment, he had seemed ill at ease in his position, because there had still been several veterans like Maigret in charge of the different departments.

He had made an effort to take on the tone of the house, as the Police Judiciaire had once been called, a tone that was hard to define: gruff and familiar, dispensing with pointless courtesies, based on mutual trust.

Not so long ago, there hadn't been many graduates, just people who had more or less seen it all as far as human beings were concerned. People who weren't surprised by anything – or angered by anything either.

They had had the worst criminals sitting in front of them and had often seen them weep. They had also seen men risk their lives to arrest other criminals who would be released by the courts and then offend again.

'I've sent for you three times this morning, Maigret.'

'So I've just been told.'

'You weren't in your office.'

The commissioner didn't know where to look, and his hand shook as he lit a cigarette.

'I thought your men were giving priority to the jewel thieves and their latest exploit on Avenue Victor-Hugo.'

'That's right.'

'It's eleven thirty now.'

He was wearing a waistcoat with a pocket watch on a chain.

'Allow me to ask you where you spent the morning.'

It was harder than in the prefect's office. First of all, it was happening at Quai des Orfèvres and not in a place that, for Maigret, was almost anonymous. He had often been in this office in his shirtsleeves, chatting to commissioners who were old colleagues and friends.

Blutet, in addition, wasn't playing his part well.

'I went to see the dentist.'

'I assume you chose one in your local area?'

'Am I obliged to answer that, sir? Until now, apart from yesterday, I've conducted many interrogations, but never been subjected to one. I had no idea we had to provide the names and addresses of our dentists, our doctors, perhaps our tailors, too.'

'I understand you.'

'You do?' he retorted ironically.

'I can put myself in your shoes, believe me. At the moment it's quite painful for me to be in my own shoes. I'm only acting on orders that have come to me from higher up. What would you answer if I asked for your whereabouts hour by hour since yesterday afternoon?'

'I'd give you my resignation.'

'Try to understand the position I'm in. You're perfectly well aware of all the stir the press are making about these jewel raids that have been happening with almost arrogant regularity in the last two months.'

'More than half took place on the Riviera and in Deauville, outside our jurisdiction.'

'Carried out by the same gang! Or at any rate, using the same methods. The last raid took place yesterday morning. Did you visit the scene, as you usually do?'

'No.'

'Have you read your inspectors' reports?'

'No.'

'Do you have any leads?'

'I've been following the same lead since these raids started up again.'

'Without any results?'

'I don't have any evidence yet, that's true. I'm waiting for them to be careless, to make a mistake, to do something apparently trivial that'll give me a chance to make a move.'

'This morning, you went to see a dentist – not your own dentist, but one in Rue des Acacias – even though your teeth are perfectly healthy. Do you suspect this dentist of having something to do with the jewel raids?'

'No.'

'Your second visit was to the building opposite.'

'Where one of my informers lives.'

'Did you talk to him about the jewel raids?'

'No.'

'Listen to me, Maigret. You know that when I started here, I had the greatest admiration for you as a man and as a police officer. Nothing has changed. But today I'm obliged, as I said, to play a role I don't like. Yesterday, you were summoned by the prefect of police. He spoke to you about an affair that's none of my business. I know only the broad outlines, and that's all I need to know. Before leaving you, he insisted that you take no part in this affair in any way whatsoever, not talk about it to anyone, even your colleagues and your inspectors. Is that correct?'

'Yes.'

The commissioner glanced at a sheet of paper on the desk in front of him.

'After that interview yesterday, you shut yourself in your office until about three o'clock. You then went to a little bistro in Rue de Seine called Désiré's. Soon afterwards, you were seen going into a hotel in Rue des Écoles, where you had a brief conversation with the manageress. Do these two places have any connection with the affair you were forbidden to have anything to do with?'

'Yes.'

'You then went, in the company of Inspector Janvier, to Rue des Acacias, where you spent quite a long time with a suspicious character named Manuel Palmari, whom you've sometimes used as an informer.'

'I assume I was followed by what the newspapers call the secret police, sir?'

He didn't say 'chief' as he usually did. He felt sick. To make it worse, the sun was full on him, and his face was covered in sweat.

Roland Blutet pretended not to have heard.

'When you got back to headquarters, you summoned an old inspector named Barnacle to your office and gave him an assignment. He was to photograph a particular young lady without her knowledge, a young lady whom the prefect of police . . .'

'. . . had forbidden me to have anything to do with.'

'Some time later, you're in a little bar in Rue Monsieur-le-Prince, in the company of Inspector Lucas and a porter from the Sorbonne. Did you talk about the jewel raids?'

'No.'

'Or about the young lady I mentioned?'

'Yes.'

'Was it pure coincidence that you took Madame Maigret to dinner in a restaurant on Avenue de la Grande-Armée?'

'No.'

'Or that in questioning a man named Landry you managed to get him to show you the register of a club?'

'This is all true, sir. I admit it never occurred to me to make sure that I wasn't being followed. Until now, I've always been on the other side of the fence.'

'If you're interested, I can assure you I wasn't responsible for this surveillance and that what little I know of the case I only found out this morning. The higher-ups seem to attach a great deal of importance to it. I'm a civil servant. When I'm ordered to do something, I have to see it through to the end.'

'Would you like me to make a written confession?'

'Don't make my task more difficult, Maigret. I'm not proud of it, believe me.'

'I'm quite prepared to believe you.'

'The fact remains that for twenty-four hours you assigned at least three inspectors in your department to tasks they shouldn't have been involved with. In other words, you used them for your personal convenience. I don't think any disciplinary action will be taken against these men, since they knew nothing of your interview with the prefect of police. It still remains for me to . . .'

The commissioner was feeling hot, too, and kept mopping his brow.

'It still remains for me to tell you the solution that's been suggested. You need rest. You've been working very hard lately, without taking any leave. You're to request a period

121

of sick leave which will last until the disciplinary investigation into your actions has been completed.'

He had got to the end only with difficulty. He no longer dared look at the man sitting in front of him. He felt embarrassed, the way you feel with an animal you have tried to kill and have merely succeeded in wounding.

'It probably won't take more than a few days. According to regulations, you'll have every opportunity to defend yourself. I believe you've already presented your version of events.'

Maigret got heavily to his feet.

'Thank you, sir.'

Then, much to the commissioner's surprise, he walked over to the nearest window.

'I assume we can open them again?'

He opened them one by one, taking the time to breathe in the warm air from outside, to see human beings moving about in the familiar setting of Paris.

'Your leave begins as of now, is that clear?'

He nodded and left the room. The commissioner didn't hold out his hand, but held it slightly in front of his body, ready to take Maigret's if the latter made a move.

Maigret didn't make that move. Nor did he collapse into an armchair in his office, as he had the day before, but went straight to the inspectors' room.

'Lucas! Janvier!'

He didn't see Barnacle.

'Come in, boys. You're going to be working without me for a while.'

Janvier understood immediately and turned pale, his

jaws clenched so tightly that he could not have uttered a word.

'I'm tired, perhaps sick. The administration, like the good mother it is, is concerned about my health and is allowing me some rest.'

He walked up and down in order not to let his closest colleagues see that his eyes were moist.

'You'll continue dealing with the jewel raids. You both know what I think of that case. And you know how stubborn I am.'

His pipe had gone out, and he put it in the big glass ashtray and filled another.

'The higher-ups know all your actions since yesterday. Mine, too, of course. Make sure to warn Barnacle as soon as he gets back. It's likely you'll both be followed as I was and as I'll continue to be. It wouldn't do me any good, quite the contrary, if any disciplinary action were taken against you. So forget everything you know about this business.'

He smiled at them.

'There, I've finished. It wasn't as hard for me as it was for the commissioner just now.'

He walked over to the armchair, where he had left his hat.

'See you later, boys.'

Janvier was the first to get his voice back.

'You know, chief . . .'

'Yes?'

'I went to the Clou Doré. I showed the photograph. Nobody there knows her.'

'It doesn't matter any more.'

'Are you giving up?'

He looked at them in turn.

'Is that how well you know me?'

'You mean you're going to continue on your own, without any back-up, even though you're under surveillance?'

'I'm going to try.'

They were both smiling now with emotion, no longer knowing what to do, how to express what they felt.

'Come on. Don't get all sentimental on me . . . I'll see you soon.'

He cut short the handshakes and headed for the door. A few moments later, he was descending the grand staircase of the Police Judiciaire.

As he passed through the arch, the two sentries saluted him, and he returned their salute with a touch of irony. It was odd to suddenly see the world through new eyes, the eyes of a free man.

He had nothing to do, no reason to turn right rather than left.

Maybe it would be one of the anglers on the banks of the river who would abandon his line and follow him. Or the driver of a grey car parked a hundred metres away.

He chose to turn right. He seemed no different from any other day as he entered the Brasserie Dauphine, where the owner came up to him as usual and shook his hand.

'Everything all right, Monsieur Maigret?'

'Oh, yes!'

'What'll you have?'

'I wonder . . .'

He felt like a different drink, not an ordinary aperitif. He remembered something from his early days in Paris. They had launched a new drink at the time, one that had been his favourite aperitif for a year or two.

'Is it still possible to get mandarin-curaçao?'

'Oh, yes. I don't get asked for it often, and young people don't know what it is, but we always keep a bottle on our shelves . . . A twist of lemon?'

He drank two, but it didn't taste quite as it used to. Then he walked slowly to the Châtelet and waited for his bus. He was in no hurry.

'Are you very sad?' Madame Maigret asked, laying the table. She had been surprised to see her husband come home so early.

'No. It was a hard blow at the time, harder than with the prefect, I'm not too sure why, maybe because it was happening in the house. Right now, I feel as if my hands have been untied, and that's rather a relief.'

'Aren't you afraid?'

'All I risk is disciplinary action, and the worst that could happen is that I'll be made to take early retirement.'

'I'm not talking about that. The people you're trying to unmask . . .'

'They can't do anything else where I'm concerned without proving me right. The chief said more than he should this morning. He told me: "Your teeth are perfectly healthy." If it wasn't for that, I'd have thought he'd got his information from the men tasked with following me. But they didn't see the inside of my mouth. Even our dentist, Ajoupa, couldn't state categorically that my teeth were healthy this morning, because he hasn't seen me for more than a year. That means that as soon as I left his surgery, Dr Mélan made a phone call, probably to Nicole Prieur. She then complained again to her uncle. The same merry-go-round as yesterday morning: the minister of the interior, the prefect of police and finally the commissioner. If you look at these things with a bit of detachment, it's all quite amusing.'

'What are you going to do with yourself?'

'Carry on.'

'Alone?'

'You're never completely alone. To start with, I'm going to call good old Pardon. He must be back from his house calls.'

Soon afterwards, he heard Dr Pardon say:

'I've just got home and was about to eat.'

'The thing is, Pardon, I need you again.'

He had, in fact, often called Pardon for medical information, or to find out about one of his colleagues.

Even when they don't know each other personally, it is quite easy for doctors to find out about each other. Graduating from the same schools, they always have a friend who was so-and-so's fellow student, professor, former hospital colleague.

It's a relatively closed circle, and in addition, they meet each other at conferences.

'This time, it's a dentist, or rather, as his brass name-plate says, a "specialist in oral medicine".'

'Personally, I don't know many.'

'His name is François Mélan, he's thirty-eight years old, and he lives and practises in a mansion in Rue des Acacias.'

There was a silence at the other end.

'Do you know him?'

'No, I was calculating . . . The question of age again . . . Thirty-eight is already another generation. It won't be easy for me to find someone among the professors who knows him.'

'Could it be done quickly?'

'With any luck, I can make a few phone calls. The first one could just as easily turn out to be the right one as the last. I also have to consult my yearbooks. Is this an important case?'

'For me personally, very important. Do you have any plans for this evening?'

He heard Pardon ask his wife:

'Do you have any plans for this evening?'

He even heard Madame Pardon reply in the background:

'You said yesterday you might take me to the cinema . . .'

'No, no plans,' Pardon said into the phone.

'What about the cinema?'

'You heard, did you? I'm not bothered about the cinema.'

'Would you both like to come over for dinner? The three of you, if your daughter's still with you.'

'No, her husband's back.'

'See you this evening, then?'

'See you this evening. If I get the information earlier, should I phone you at your office?'

'I don't have an office any more.'

'What? Are you serious?'

'Let's just say that until further orders, I'm a private citizen again, without any privileges or responsibilities.'

It was like a Sunday afternoon, except that around him Paris was living its weekday life, and the noises and the smells and the light were not those of a Sunday.

After lunch, he dozed off in his armchair without realizing it. On opening his eyes, he was surprised to see that it was 3.30.

'I was fast asleep,' he observed in a thick voice.

'You even snored. Would you like a cup of coffee?'

'I'd love one.'

He needed to get his thoughts back in order, but he refused to think about the case, preferring to let it settle inside him.

What could he try to do? Almost nothing. In all likelihood, someone was keeping an eye on him outside on Boulevard Richard-Lenoir, ready to follow him wherever he went.

There was no question of going to Boulevard de Courcelles, let alone waiting for Nicole Prieur when she left her classes. She would be quite capable of calling for help, and he would find himself in a ridiculous position.

Would they even let him go and see Dr Mélan again? It was unlikely. He wasn't even sure he would have access to Manuel's apartment. As for phoning him, that was impossible: he himself had ordered that Manuel's telephone be tapped.

'I added sugar. Careful, it's very hot.'

She was looking at her husband with a touch of anxiety, and he smiled at her good-naturedly.

'Don't worry, Madame Maigret. Your old husband will make it.'

He only called her Madame Maigret when he was in a cheerful mood, and she was quite surprised.

'You seem calm.'

'I am.'

'Seeing you like this, anyone would think you didn't have any problems.'

'That's because they're bound to be solved.'

'Are you going out?'

'I'm taking a little walk.'

'Are you sure you're not in any danger?'

'I could be knocked down by a bus or a car, like anyone else.'

There was nevertheless an emotional undertone. He sipped at his coffee.

'Have you done the shopping for dinner?'

'I phoned and had everything delivered. Do you want to know what we're eating?'

'I'd rather be surprised.'

He hadn't walked a hundred metres along the street before he turned and spotted the men following him. There were two of them, and they immediately began gesticulating as they talked as if they were in the midst of a passionate argument.

Maigret didn't know them. They probably belonged to a department attached directly to the Ministry of the Interior.

He went as far as the Bastille, thought of shaking off the two men, just for the pleasure of playing a trick on them, then gave up the idea with a shrug.

He sat for almost an hour on a café terrace, like a man of independent means, reading the evening newspapers, which he had just bought from a newsstand.

He returned home via Boulevard Beaumarchais and Rue du Chemin-Vert. As he still had time to kill, he took a shower and spruced himself up.

Pardon hadn't phoned. He and his wife arrived at eight o'clock, and they sat down to eat immediately. There was soufflé as a starter, followed by coq au vin.

'It took me a while, but by chance I came across someone who knows your man well. I'll tell you about it later.'

'Do you remember what we were saying at our last dinner at your place? The spiteful criminal? Wickedness for its own sake? I'm thinking now I might have been wrong.'

He didn't want to talk any more about it over the meal. Coffee was served in the sitting room, and the two men took theirs into the little study Maigret had set up for himself.

'Would you excuse us, ladies?'

'What would you like, sloe gin or raspberry liqueur?'

Pardon replied, as if speaking for both of them:

'Neither.'

The window was open, and night was starting to fall, just like during their last conversation, except that this time the air was still and the sky clear, without any threat of a storm.

'It was the fifth or sixth person I called who reminded me of a man I knew quite well years ago. Actually I knew his sister rather better. I even think that when I was about eighteen I was vaguely tempted to marry her. I'd completely lost sight of the two of them. It so happens that this man, Vivier, lives not far from me, on Boulevard Voltaire. I was able to get him alone for a while between patients. He's a professor of oral medicine and he knows François Mélan very well. Young Mélan, as he calls him, was a student of his.'

Pardon threw Maigret a long look and asked:

'Are you very interested in him? Is this a criminal matter?'

To which Maigret replied, slowly:

'Either I'm mistaken and within a week I'll be retiring to Meung-sur-Loire or I'm right and I'm dealing with the most curious case in my career.'

'And this case revolves around Mélan?'

'Yes.'

'It's odd.'

'What is?'

'There are some similarities between what you just said and what Vivier told me. Have you been to see Mélan?'

'This morning, pretending I had a toothache.'

'Is he tall, short-sighted, with red hair, blue eyes and long arms?'

'I didn't notice how long his arms were.'

'What did he tell you?'

'That I had healthy teeth.'

'The first thing to know about him is that he's from a

very poor background. His father was a day labourer in a village on the Somme. The family was pretty much the poorest of all, and what's more, the father would get drunk every Saturday. There were five children. François Mélan had, and probably still has, a sister who's two or three years older than him. All this Vivier only found out a long time after meeting his student. For two years, he knew almost nothing about him. Mélan isn't the kind of man who confides in people. He didn't have any friends. Nobody knew of any relationships with women. In the faculty, nobody knew that he worked at night to pay for his studies, and Vivier still wonders where he did his secondary education and in what circumstances. I'll try and quote what he said verbatim: "A gifted young man, highly intelligent, but withdrawn in character, and probably tormented".'

Maigret listened as if filing each word away in his brain.

'In the end, Vivier took him on as his assistant, not just to do him a favour, but because he was his best pupil. "It was hard at first," he told me. "It isn't easy to have an assistant who doesn't say a word outside the department, someone whose private life you don't know anything about. One evening, I invited him home, and he took a lot of persuading. After dinner, I took him into my office and tried my best to get him to talk. We'd been drinking wine, and now I served cognac. He was quite reluctant to try it. Gradually, though, he livened up, and I found out a few things about his past." '

Pardon lit a cigar and looked at Maigret again.

'Does this still fit with what you know?'

'I'm eager to hear the rest.'

'It's both simple and tragic. In the faculty, Mélan's fellow students had dubbed him the Virgin. There was even a rumour that he had homosexual tendencies. The story he told Vivier explains his behaviour. He was fourteen, unless I'm mistaken, when the Germans invaded. His family was too poor to take to the roads and escape like so many others. One evening, Mélan and his sister were at the side of the road when two men on motorcycles appeared. They were the first German soldiers they'd seen. They stopped to ask them the way to some village or other. Then they said something to each other and laughed. Finally, they motioned to the girl to lie down on the embankment and when she hesitated they forced her down. Both of them had their way with her and then left, laughing at the boy, who hadn't moved. Seeing the sexual act for the first time in such circumstances could well have produced a trauma in a sensitive child. "Is it because of that memory that we never see you with girls?" Vivier asked. Mélan was embarrassed. "I don't know," he replied. "I may get married one day like anybody else. Though I wonder if I'll dare, if I'm capable of making a woman happy."'

There was a silence. Maigret was so solemn that Pardon spoke first.

'Do you think he's committed a crime?'

Maigret didn't reply immediately.

'Until now, I wasn't thinking of a real crime. Now, I'm almost certain of it. Did the professor tell you anything else?'

'Not about Mélan, but about his female assistant, who worked for Vivier for a time. Have you met her?'

'Yes.'

'Is it true she's very ugly?'

'Even worse than that.'

'She's thought of as a nasty piece of work, those are the words Vivier used. Actually, she's the most sensitive and most devoted young woman, and in her neighbourhood she's the one people go to when there's a sick or dying person to keep an eye on.'

'What is her neighbourhood?'

'I didn't ask. I could phone Vivier and inquire after the address.'

8.

Maigret was impressively calm. Nothing of what was happening inside him appeared on the surface, except that he had acquired a new weight, a new density. This was the first time Pardon had seen him at a time when the threads of an investigation were starting to come together, when the truth was gradually taking shape, and he observed his friend as if trying to discover the wheels turning behind that heavy, expressionless face.

'What kind of man is Vivier? Is he broad-minded?'

'Except when you mention state interference in the organization of medical services. Then he's one of the angriest of protesters, a fanatical individualist.'

Puffing slowly on his pipe, Maigret remained silent, but without giving the impression that he was thinking. Rather, he seemed absent, and it was a surprise to see him subsequently resume the conversation at the exact point where he had left off.

'Is there any chance we'd find him at home?'

'He's working on a big treatise on oral medicine. It's going to be his life's work, and he spends part of his nights on it.'

'Could you phone him and ask him if he'd mind my having a word with him?'

Within a few moments, Pardon had Vivier on the line.

'Pardon here. I'm calling you from the apartment of my friend Detective Chief Inspector Maigret and I apologize for disturbing you while you're working. The inspector would like to speak to you for a moment.'

The answer must have been funny, because Pardon smiled.

'Of course. I'll pass him to you.'

He held the receiver out to Maigret.

'I also apologize for disturbing you, professor. If you would agree to answer two or three questions, you would greatly ease my task . . . Yes, Pardon told me all about your conversation, which is of enormous interest to me . . . I should emphasize that I'm calling you in a private capacity. I'm on indefinite sick leave . . . No, I'm not ill, or, if I am, it must be very serious, because my friend Pardon, who's my doctor, assures me my health is perfect. The truth of the matter is, an investigation I'm involved in has brought me up against some people with influential contacts, and as I'm in the habit of seeing things through to the end, I've been strongly advised to rest for a few days . . . This is my first question, professor. Would you be very surprised to learn that your former assistant, Dr Mélan, has committed one or several criminal acts?'

At the other end of the line, there was a kind of bark that could have passed for a laugh. When Vivier spoke, it was in the sonorous voice of a man who has his own opinions and expresses them vigorously.

'I wouldn't be all that surprised, my dear inspector, if I was told the same thing about myself, or you, or my concierge. Under sufficient external or internal pressure, anybody is capable of committing acts that are condemned by the law and morality.'

'In his case, do you think the pressure would be more likely to be internal than external?'

'Have you met him?'

'This morning, for a few minutes.'

'Has Pardon repeated to you what I told him about Mélan?'

'Yes, just now.'

'And what's your opinion?'

'I'd rather hear yours.'

'Internal pressure, indisputably! Mélan is the classic introvert who doesn't allow his emotions to appear on the surface. Apart from one or two conversations when I was able to get him to talk about himself – and it wasn't easy – he's probably never confided in anyone.'

'Assuming he has committed a crime, any crime, would you say he might not have been fully responsible for his actions?'

'Are you asking me as a doctor or as a man? As a doctor, that's not my speciality. I'd leave it to the psychiatrists to pronounce on that, and their judgement would depend on the circumstances.'

He added, ironically:

'On the age of the psychiatrists, too, and what school they belong to.'

'And as a man?'

'Personally, knowing him as I do, I'd happily be a witness for the defence.'

'My second question is more difficult to formulate and

I fear it may surprise you. Would a man like Mélan, feeling cornered, react in a simple or a complicated manner?'

'Good heavens, Monsieur Maigret, you seem to know him almost as well as I do. In a complicated manner, obviously! And even then, the word "complicated" is an understatement. When he was working with me, Mélan always chose – in everything, even in answering an exam question – the most complex path. He had the very opposite of what I'd call a one-track mind. He grasps all the possibilities, all the possible ramifications of a subject and makes sure he doesn't neglect any aspect.'

'Many thanks. There's just one favour I need to ask you, if you think you can do it and if you trust me. It's quite possible I'm mistaken, that the theory I'm constructing right now will turn out to be wrong before the night is out. But if the facts confirm it, several people are in grave danger. A conversation with Mademoiselle Motte would probably suffice to clarify that point. I assume she has a telephone. If you can get her to see me tonight, either at home or anywhere else, it's quite likely we can avoid further tragedies.'

'So poor Motte scares you, too? When I think that everyone would consider her an angel if she didn't look so off-putting! I'll phone her. What number should I call you back on?'

Maigret stood up and went into the sitting room, where the two women had been whispering in order not to disturb them.

'I think I'll have a drop of sloe gin after all. Unless Pardon grabs the glass out of my hands . . .'

Pardon did nothing of the sort. He was still studying

his friend with a mixture of admiration and curiosity, not entirely devoid of fear.

He was wondering what had set Maigret off on these hypotheses and would have liked to reconstruct the progress of his thoughts.

'Hello? . . . Yes, professor, this is Maigret . . . She's agreed to see me right away? I hope it wasn't too difficult? . . . A little? . . . May I ask her address? . . . Rue des Francs-Bourgeois, yes . . . Yes, I know the building. I lived not far from there for a while, on Place des Vosges . . . I'm very grateful to you . . . Yes . . . I'd like to meet you, too.'

When he stood up, he was still as calm as ever, but there was a little gleam in his eyes that hadn't been there before.

'You won't be too upset, Pardon, if I leave you with the ladies? By the way, there's a good chance my phone is being tapped. It's possible the people who are taking an interest in what I'm doing might get there before me. There are probably one or two inspectors from Special Branch out there in the street, pacing up and down.'

'Why don't I drive you? I have my car. I can be back in a few minutes.'

They went into the sitting room.

'Are you going out? Will you be gone for long?'

'I have no idea what time I'll be back.'

'Isn't it a bit risky?'

'Not at this stage, not any more. Pardon will drive me and then come straight back.'

On the way, he didn't utter a word. There was no car following them. Had they relaxed their surveillance, knowing he was with the Pardons?

Rue des Francs-Bourgeois, in the Marais, still had a few historic mansions that now housed a host of poor households, mostly of small artisans, many originally from Poland, Hungary or the former Lithuania.

'Goodnight, Pardon, and thanks. If I succeed, I'll owe it in large part to you.'

'Good luck.'

Maigret rang the doorbell. The unseen concierge pressed something to open a little door embedded in the carriage entrance, and he crossed what had once been some great nobleman's main courtyard.

'Mademoiselle Motte, please?'

Through a skylight, a voice replied:

'Second floor on the left. First door.'

The light came on as he started up the stairs, and he saw Dr Mélan's assistant leaning over the banister. When he came level with her, she whispered:

'I thought you might not find your way. The building is quite complicated.'

She looked different in a dark dress from the way she'd looked in her uniform, more vulnerable somehow. There was anxiety in her deep-set eyes. The emotion had brought out red blotches on her excessively white skin.

'This way. Hurry up, the light will be going out soon.'

She admitted him to a very clean, almost cheerful room, which served as both sitting room and dining room; its provincial furniture, which had accrued a patina over time, contributed a peaceful, reassuring note.

'Sit down. I don't mind if you smoke.'

'I hope the professor didn't wake you?'

'I don't sleep much.'

There was no radio or television in sight, but there were lots of books on the shelves, and one open beside an armchair.

'Have you forgotten your pipe?'

She made no attempt to give him a welcoming smile, or to hide her anxieties.

'I realized when I saw you in the waiting room this morning that things were taking a bad turn. What surprises me is that you've come here.'

'As I told Professor Vivier, mademoiselle, I'm here in a private capacity. I have no right to pester you. My superiors have put me on sick leave in order to avoid any bother to some influential people. You would have been perfectly entitled to shut the door in my face, which is why I asked Professor Vivier for help. I know you trust him. Even now, you have the right not to answer my questions.'

He was speaking slowly, in a low voice, almost as if he were unsure of himself.

'The day before yesterday, I was the object of a plot carefully mounted against me, a trap so subtle I was almost certain to fall into it.'

Barely two days ago! All the incidents that had happened since then were jumbled up in Maigret's memory, those that were important and those that were less so: Manuel's wheelchair, the stains on the walls of the mansion opposite, the Spanish maid's black hair, the doctor's blue eyes, grossly enlarged by his glasses, just a few centimetres from Maigret's face . . .

When the time was right, every detail would take its

place, as well as its meaning, its significance within the whole picture.

'There is only ever one truth,' Maigret liked to say. 'The difficult thing is to recognize it, to flush it from where it lurks.'

'Would you like a cup of coffee?'

'No, thank you. You're anxious to know why exactly I'm here. I've now learned enough about Dr Mélan's past to understand his behaviour.'

She was looking at him even more attentively than Pardon had earlier, her hands folded in her lap.

'The person who set that trap for me was desperate. His tendency, when faced with a problem, is to look for the subtlest, most complicated solution. Strangely, it took an almost miraculous combination of circumstances for me to become interested in his actions.'

Her eyes wide open, she stammered in astonishment:

'Haven't you had the doctor under surveillance for several weeks?'

'No, mademoiselle. The person I had under surveillance is a gangster who lives in the building opposite, and the men you spotted in the street were there to find out who was visiting him and to follow his mistress when she went out.'

'I still can't . . .'

'I know, you can't believe it. And yet it's the truth. Lately, I myself paid several visits to this person, whose name is Manuel Palmari, and, as is an old habit of mine, I occasionally went and stood by the window.'

'So you weren't there because of . . .'

'Because of Dr Mélan? I didn't even know his name. The only reason I might have looked as if I was taking an interest in his mansion is that I have a weakness for old houses. I was, as I've said, the victim of a plot. Someone tried to get me out of the way. Someone who, instead of using strongarm tactics, constructed a complicated, almost diabolical plan, in which there was no flaw. Suspecting Manuel of certain crimes and having had my eye on him for a long time, I began by thinking it was him and went to see him several times. I also learned that Mademoiselle Prieur, who played an important role in the affair, was a member of a club on Avenue de la Grande-Armée. In the register of that club, I found the name of your employer as one of the young lady's sponsors and I decided I'd like to take a look at him.'

'It's incredible.'

She wasn't questioning what Maigret was saying, she was stunned at the unpredictable workings of fate.

'Dr Mélan could have played the game, drilled into a tooth that didn't need it, even taken it out. Instead of which, he told me honestly that I had healthy teeth and walked me to the door without a word, without a question.'

'He was terrified. For some weeks now, he's been living in a state of constant panic.'

'Did he tell you that?'

'No, but I know him well enough to be aware of it. So was Carola.'

'The maid? Is she his mistress?'

'He doesn't have a mistress. Carola sleeps right at the top of the house, in the attic, even though there are more rooms than we know what to do with.'

'Do you understand why I'm here, mademoiselle?'

'To question me.'

'Not exactly, because I don't even know what questions to ask you. I've tried to be honest with you. As I said, I don't have any authority at this moment. Nor am I certain about anything, and my hypotheses are still quite vague. Nobody could have dreamed up that plot against me without having a vital interest in doing so, unless they hated me personally. But although Dr Mélan may know me by name, he'd never met me before this morning. And yet the fact that I was in the apartment opposite, after my inspectors had been seen in the street, terrified him. Why? What could be so powerful as to make him want to get me out of the way?

'That was my starting point. What could I have found out about him that was serious enough to explain what he did? Here, too, chance played a part. Manuel's mistress, Aline, had a toothache for the first time in her life, so naturally she went to see the dentist opposite. She may not be intelligent, but she has uncommonly sharp intuition. She's very much a woman. Mélan asked her two little questions too many, or rather, if I remember correctly, you asked the first one: "Who sent you here?" That's a question a dentist or his secretary rarely asks a patient. The second one was: "Do you have anything else wrong with you?"

'Aline was so struck by the atmosphere in the house that her brain started working. She remembered the light she often saw in the surgery in the evening. When I questioned her, she replied that after nightfall, only women, not men, came to the door.'

'I wasn't there after nightfall.'

'I know. You must have known about those visits, though.'

'Listen, inspector. I agreed to see you because of Professor Vivier. All the same, I want you to know that I'll do anything in the world to prevent anything happening to Dr Mélan. He's a man who's suffered all his life, who's suffering more than ever, who'll always suffer. He had a particularly painful childhood.'

'I know the incident you're referring to.'

'What incident? He never mentioned any incident. He doesn't confide in anyone.'

'Early in the war, his sister—'

'I didn't know he had a sister.'

Maigret told her about the rape, and her eyes opened wide again.

'That may explain lots of things.'

'I can tell you that, whatever happens, according to Professor Vivier, the psychiatrists will find that he wasn't entirely responsible for his actions. Vivier has already agreed to appear as a witness for the defence. And I may do so, too.'

'You?'

'Yes, me. But I need your help. You admit that he's living in fear. A large proportion of crimes are committed out of fear.'

'They'll put him in prison all the same. And he's not the kind of man who could bear prison.'

'I've heard that said of all the people I've ever arrested. You know as well as I do that the doctor performed abortions, don't you?'

'I realized that the day I looked in a drawer and found a probe and other objects he shouldn't have needed.'

'Any other clue?'

'I refuse to make things worse for him.'

'Do you want to know what I think, mademoiselle? Tell me first of all if Mélan is a Christian.'

'He doesn't practise any religion.'

'In that case, as far as he's concerned, abortion isn't necessarily a serious offence. It's a matter of morality, which varies from place to place, country to country. Some accept it, others condemn it. You see, if it was only that, I don't think your employer would be in such a panic as to act the way he's acted in the past few days. Hasn't that occurred to you?'

'Yes.'

'Why?'

She turned her head away, and, after a fairly long silence, stammered:

'You're asking me to do a terrible thing. I'm all he has.'

'What do you mean?'

'That he's always been alone . . . Totally alone . . . I know he goes out, I know he goes to that club you mentioned. That's to find some kind of reassurance, perhaps also to . . .'

'To recruit patients?'

'I did think of that.'

'What about Nicole Prieur?'

'I suspect that the first time she came, it was for the same thing as the others.'

'The other evening visitors, you mean?'

'Yes. I don't have a file card made out in her name. She's

a hysterical girl who threw herself at him. I'm sure she's the one doing the pursuing.'

'Is she his mistress?'

Another silence.

'Shall I answer that for you?' Maigret suggested. 'You're convinced that Mélan has never had a mistress, any more now than when he was a student and his classmates called him the Virgin.'

'I didn't know that.'

'Am I right?'

'It did occur to me.'

'And so, just like me, you suspected something else.'

She stood up, almost at the end of her tether, and paced up and down the room.

'You're torturing me.'

'Would you rather there were further crimes?'

She suddenly looked him in the eyes, terrified.

'How did you find out all this? Has Carola talked?'

'Does Carola know?'

'All right, it seems I have to go all the way. I can't keep this secret much longer. As soon as I began working for Dr Mélan, I was surprised that he kept me out of his surgery when he saw female patients.'

'You mean the daytime patients?'

'Obviously. I wasn't there in the evening.'

'All of the female patients?'

'No. With some of them – with the male patients, too, although there weren't many of those – I did what a dental nurse usually does, handing the doctor the instruments he needed, preparing the X-rays and so on.'

'But, for some female patients, you were sent back to your office?'

'Yes.'

'Without any explanation?'

'Dr Mélan never explains anything.'

'Did you suspect something?'

'Because of a newspaper article. In the United States, in Connecticut, I think, there was a dentist who, when a female patient struck him as desirable, had no compunction about increasing the anaesthetic.'

'Another shy man, probably, who had neither a wife nor a mistress . . .'

'Yes.'

'What happened recently to make you certain?'

'A patient went in and didn't come back out. I was surprised, because they all come through my office on the way out. He told me he'd shown her out down the little staircase.'

'And Carola says he didn't?'

'That's right. Her kitchen looks out on that staircase, and the door is always open. Apart from that . . .'

'Go on.'

'Nothing . . . I can't . . .'

'Let me help you again. Does Dr Mélan have a gardener?'

'No.'

'Does he do the gardening himself?'

'Not very much. There are more weeds there than flowers.'

'You asked Carola if, that night—'

'No. She was the one who mentioned it to me.'

'And you haven't told this to anyone?'

'No. He's alone. He thinks he's ugly.'

She was alone. She was ugly.

'Was that the only accident?'

'To the best of my knowledge.'

'But you aren't there when he sees the evening patients. Is Carola in the house then?'

'She sometimes goes to the cinema.'

'So other accidents may have occurred.'

'It's not impossible.'

'And there may be more in the future.'

'What do you want me to do?'

'I want you to help me. I'm not allowed to go to Rue des Acacias, where the police would stop me from going in. Besides, if I did go there, it's quite possible that Mélan might put a bullet in his head. Does he have a gun?'

'Yes. An old army revolver.'

'Call him and say you have something serious and urgent to tell him, something it's best not to discuss on the phone. Ask him to come here. I assume he has his car. And he trusts you.'

'What if he brings his revolver?'

'He wouldn't do that to come and see you.'

'Then he'll have nobody left, not even me . . .'

'Think of the woman or women whose remains will probably be found in the garden.'

'I understand . . . It's hard all the same . . . Why should it be me? . . . If you're a Catholic, it reminds you of something, doesn't it?'

And when he shook his head, she said:

'Judas!'

Slowly, she walked over to the telephone. Her thin fingers dialled the number. The red patches had faded from her face, and her eyes were half shut.

'Is that you, doctor? This is Motte.'

From the moment she hung up, she didn't utter a word. Nor did Maigret. They sat face to face, without looking at each other, waiting. Twice, Maigret had to relight his pipe because he had forgotten to inhale.

Both had to make an effort of will not to pace up and down the room to kill time.

Every now and again, Maigret looked at his watch. Mademoiselle Motte could see the time on the clock over his head, which he heard ticking.

The time seemed to drag. Would Mélan come? If he had realized that it was all up for him, he might already have put a bullet in his head. But Carola would no doubt have heard the shot, and her first reaction would have been to phone Mademoiselle Motte before informing the police, whom she seemed to have no liking for.

Carola might be at the cinema. And what if tonight Nicole Prieur . . . For her part, Mademoiselle Motte must be asking herself pretty much the same questions. Through the half-open window, the few sounds of the street could be heard: a car gliding past, the occasional passer-by, a couple whose voices could be made out . . .

It seemed an eternity, although in fact only twenty minutes had passed, twenty minutes of silence and stillness.

A car stopping. A slight screech of brakes. Footsteps on

the pavement, followed by a muffled, distant ringing. The little door closing within the larger one. Steps on the uneven cobblestones of the courtyard, the glass door opening in its turn, the stairs . . .

Mademoiselle Motte put her hand on her chest and muttered to herself:

'I can't . . .'

Seeing her stand up, he thought she was going to rush into the kitchen to hide, or perhaps escape down another staircase. Once on her feet, she didn't move, and he now stood up, too, as tense as she was.

It was so silent that they heard the slight click of the time switch in the corridor. The light had just gone out. A hand groped for the door, and Mademoiselle Motte went and opened it.

Mélan was wearing a grey suit and holding his hat in his hand. He advanced one metre inside, turned without having seen Maigret, looked at Mademoiselle Motte, opened his mouth, then, turning again, discovered Maigret.

He didn't speak immediately. Nor did he try to rush outside. In spite of his surprise, his emotion, it was clear that he was trying to understand, that his brain was working fast.

The problem must have struck him as a hard one to solve. After a while, he shook his head, as if wiping an equation from the blackboard to start again from scratch. All his faculties were stretched to breaking point.

Now, he looked at them in turn, his brow furrowed, then at the armchairs in which they had been sitting, the pipe in the ashtray, within reach of Maigret's hand.

'Have you been here long?' he asked at last, his voice almost calm.

'Quite long.'

His blue eyes lingered on Mademoiselle Motte's pained face. They expressed neither anger nor indignation. Surprise, certainly, but above all, a question . . . a question . . . a question . . .

He needed to understand . . . He wanted to understand . . . He had an exceptional brain . . . He had always been told he had an exceptional brain . . . He had proved it . . . He had started from the bottom . . . right at the bottom . . . and he . . .

'It wasn't her, doctor,' Maigret said to put an end to this painful scene. 'When I came in here, I already knew everything, or almost everything. I just needed confirmation.'

There was no hatred in Mélan's eyes as he stared at Maigret. What had Pardon asked him, during their last dinner in Rue Popincourt? A crime of spite, consciously prepared . . . Wickedness for its own sake . . .

For a while, Maigret had thought he had encountered it for the first time in his career . . .

But Mélan didn't hate him. Mélan didn't hate anybody. He was afraid. Perhaps he had been afraid all his life . . .

'I phoned Professor Vivier.'

Mélan's astonishment grew, but he didn't say a word, and it was only his eyes that expressed this astonishment, magnified by his glasses.

'He'll be a witness for the defence. I might be one, too.'

Epilogue

Twenty minutes later, Mélan's car drew up outside the main police station of the third arrondissement in Rue Perrée. Maigret was the first to get out.

When they entered the corridor, it was the dentist's turn to walk in front. 'Carry on. Second door on the left.'

One of the inspectors had his feet on the table and was reading the newspaper and smoking his pipe; another was typing a report on a battered typewriter.

They both stood up on recognizing Maigret.

'Good evening, gentlemen. I'm sorry to disturb you. I'm not here officially. I've just brought Dr Mélan, who would like to make a statement. I assume you'll be the one to type it, Bassin?'

He had known him for twenty years.

'It's possible that once the statement has been signed, you'll have to take the doctor to the cells at headquarters. Treat him gently. No rough stuff. Goodnight, doctor.'

By the time Maigret got home, the Pardons had left. Madame Maigret wasn't in bed.

'Well?'

'He's confessing right now.'

'What?'

'Everything. Everything that's on his mind. We'll read

about it in tomorrow's papers. The afternoon ones, it's too late for the morning editions.'

'Is he the one who's been causing you all this trouble?'

'He was scared because he'd seen me at a window and assumed I was watching him.'

'What are you going to do?'

'Wait.'

The summons came at ten in the morning, brought by an officer on a bicycle. He wasn't asked to see the prefect of police, but the commissioner of the Police Judiciaire.

'Come in.'

He opened the door, his pipe in his mouth, just as he had been coming into this same office every morning for so many years, whoever the successive occupants were.

'There you are, Maigret. Take a seat . . . What can I say?'

'Nothing, sir.'

'Sir?'

'Chief, if you prefer.'

'I do prefer . . . Are you angry with me?'

'No.'

'I phoned the prefect, who phoned the minister of the interior.'

'Who, in turn, phoned his friend Jean-Baptiste Prieur.'

'Quite likely. Janvier is waiting for you in his office. He was on duty last night. He took the call when it came in from the third arrondissement. Early this morning, he went to Rue des Acacias with a road digger. The remains of three women were dug up. The first was buried about five years ago. For the second, the pathologist says it might have been three years ago, or it might have been two. The third died less than a month ago.'

The commissioner, too, was asking himself a question. How had Maigret . . . But he didn't dare ask it out loud.

'You're back on the case, of course.'

After which, he still had to prove that Manuel was the mastermind behind the jewel raids.

They hadn't seen the last of him in Rue des Acacias.

INSPECTOR MAIGRET

NIGHT AT THE CROSSROADS

GEORGES SIMENON

She stepped forwards, her silhouette slightly blurred in the dim light. She stepped forwards like a film star, or rather, like the perfect woman of an adolescent's dream.

And her brother stood by her as a slave stands near the sovereign he is sworn to protect.

On the outskirts of Paris, a sensational crime in an isolated neighbourhood becomes the focus of Maigret's investigation. But the strange behaviour of an enigmatic Danish aristocrat and his reclusive sister prove to be even more troubling.

Translated by Linda Coverdale